SLEIGHT OF MIND

stories by

K. PATRICK GLOVER

The stories contained in this volume have appeared previously, in books, magazines, and on the web. Many first appeared on the now sadly shuttered UK based site, *Weaponizer,* a home for a wide variety of speculative fiction to which I owe a debt of thanks for their support over the years.

The final story here, *In The Court of The Yellow King,* first appeared in the Roxton anthology *In The Blink of An Eye,* featuring stories inspired by Erik Kristopher Myers' film, *Butterfly Kisses.* The story is reprinted here with his kind permission.

www.roxtonpress.com

dedication

This book is for my mother, Janice. It's for my wife, Amanda. It's for my children, Taylor, Remy, Aidan, Peter, Lily, Patrick, and Tessa. It's for my life long friends, Scott and Ed. It's for some of the new friends I've met along the way. It's for all the people who have loved me and I have loved, who have supported me through the long years as they've ticked by, who have always believed that this book would sit on their shelves one day. The first of many. Thank you, all of you.

CONTENTS

Devils and Dust

It was hot and dry and dusty that day.

It was hot and dry and dusty every day in Epitaph. There was a general consensus that the little border town lived up to its name, at least in spirit. It felt like the summation of our lives, the final word on an existence so barren of love and decency that it led us here to die.

It had been years since I had fought in the war between the north and the south. It was a war that changed everything and, in many ways, a war that changed nothing. The divide that had split our country still existed. We just didn't talk about it much anymore.

The horrors of that war had done something to those of us who survived them. Something undefinable, something that led us away from the civilized towns and cities of the booming west and to places like Epitaph.

Would I have come to Epitaph if I had known what would happen on that day? If I could somehow have glimpsed into the future and seen the cloud of death and despair? I think, even knowing the price I would pay, that I would have.

But there was no hint on that hot summer day of what was to come. No foreshadowing. That was the stuff of fiction, of dusty dime novels full of melodrama and gun smoke. Real life didn't work that way, at least not in my experience.

I had spent the day working on a fence for Lloyd Bennett and had worked up a mighty hunger, otherwise I would have gone home that night. As it was, I found myself at the Standing Horse, drinking whiskey and devouring a thick slab of steak.

Andrea, who ran the saloon, took special care with my supper each night, and it was cooked just the way I liked it. She made sure my glass was always full and often forgot to charge me for the exact number of glasses that I consumed. She was a slender girl with sharp features, but the softest eyes I had ever seen. I had sometimes thought of courting her. One more in a long line of regrets.

When I finished my supper, I sat by the back wall, drinking my whiskey and listening to the murmurs of drunken conversation that drifted from the other tables. The Standing Horse was a quiet little place, with an air of desperation that hung about like a cloud of smoke.

Nobody really wanted to be there. Nobody really wanted to be in Epitaph. Yet we had all ended up there and we were all trying, in our own weak ways, to make the best of the situation.

I don't know what it was that drew my attention to the opening door, but I wasn't the only one who stopped to look. The room, already quiet, fell completely silent as we saw the stranger standing in the doorway. He was a tall man and his visage was frightening. Time and hardship had taken its toll on him. It was impossible to tell his age.

He looked around the saloon, taking everything and everyone in, no emotion betraying his thoughts. It felt, to those of us in that room, like judgment was at hand. His gaze settled on a young cow hand who sat by himself, near the piano.

"What's your name, son?" The stranger's voice was like broken glass in the silent room. It carried a weight with it, as if it was tangible. A sound you could reach out and touch, if you dared.

"Charlie. Charlie Richards."

The stranger nodded. "Stand up, Mr. Richards."

The young man was frightened, but doing his best not to show it. "Why?" he asked.

"I aim to kill you. Best to do it with you standing and prepared." The stranger spoke deliberately and his words seemed devoid of inflection or emotion.

Charlie broke into a sweat and his own voice pitched a bit higher. "Mister, I don't even know you."

"Don't matter. Die sitting or die standing, choice is yours." Then the stranger did something that made him seem even more frightening. He smiled.

Andrea came out from behind the bar, furious. "Mister, you leave that boy alone or I'm going to get the Sheriff."

"Sheriff's dead." He turned his frightening gaze upon her. "You'll get your turn, little lady. No need to be in such a hurry to die."

Andrea stepped back, her face contorted in shock, as if she had been physically slapped. The stranger turned back to poor Charlie Richards. "Well, boy, what's it going to be? You going down like a man?"

Charlie pushed his chair back and slowly got to his feet. "I don't see why we've got to do this," he whispered.

"You don't have to understand. You're only concern now is putting a bullet in me before I put one in you."

Charlie was fast, I had seen him draw down before, but he was nowhere near fast enough to beat this man. He had barely cleared his holster when we heard the thunder erupt from the stranger's gun.

Charlie rocked back as the bullet struck him and his gun dropped to the floor. Then the pain washed over him and he clamped his hands over the spurting hole in his gut. He tried to speak, but only a gurgling noise came out.

We all watched as he tried to stagger forward and then collapsed to the floor. He lay there, not yet dead, but dying, his body convulsing. Andrea started to go to him, but the stranger shook his head.

"Leave him where he lies. It'll be over soon enough."

Nobody said a word. Most of the room watched Charlie as he bled out on the old wooden floor. I kept my eyes on the stranger, knowing that the night was far from over. I could already feel the guilt building inside me. The feeling that I should have done something.

Yet I had seen the stranger draw and I knew I couldn't beat him. I would just be another body on the floor. That's all any of us would be, there were no real gunfighters in the room. If the Sheriff was really dead, what chance did we have?

"Bring me a bottle of whiskey." The stranger's voice echoed across the room. He was looking around, searching faces for someone to challenge him. I never thought it would be Andrea.

"You can go to hell," she yelled, and threw a bottle at his head. He caught it smoothly with his left hand and as Andrea brought up a shotgun from beneath the bar, he fired with his right.

Andrea's face exploded in a mist of blood and flesh and bone and I felt a part of me die with her. I turned my head to the door, hoping the deafening gunshots had drawn some attention from outside.

The stranger looked at me and grinned. "You can stop looking at that door. No one's coming. There's no one left to help. I've killed them all."

"The whole town?" I asked, incredulous.

"Well, it's not like there was a lot of them. Barely took an hour or so." He holstered his gun and pulled the cork from the whiskey bottle. I watched him take a long pull from it then set the bottle aside, instantly forgotten.

"But, the whole town?" I couldn't get my head around the thought.

"Yes, the whole town. There's nothing outside that door but devils and dust." Hand resting on his gun, he slowly walked around the room, taking the measure of each of my fellow patrons. There were eight men left, beside myself, and not a one of them could or would hold his gaze.

He laughed in contempt at them and finally stood before my table. I looked into his eyes and saw nothing there save death, but I didn't look away. He nodded his approval.

"So," he asked, "are you the hero?"

"No, I'm just a man."

He looked me over as if he was unsure of what he had found. "There's something in your countenance. A soldier?"

I nodded. "Once upon a time."

"Union or Confederate?"

"Does it matter?"

"I suppose not. Are you armed?"

"I wear a revolver on my right thigh."

"Are you any good with it?" he asked.

"I usually hit what I'm aiming at."

"Think you could outdraw me?"

"No."

"Why don't you unhook that revolver and lay it on the table in front of you? Slowly, of course."

"Of course." I did as he asked, but lay the gun close to me, the barrel pointed in his direction. He took no notice of my precaution and I knew then that he didn't consider me a true threat.

"Colt Peacemaker," he proclaimed. "That's a lawman's piece. You a lawman?"

"No."

He studied me now, unsure if he believed my words. "Where did you get the gun?"

"Off the body of a man I killed, during the war. Seemed a shame to let it go to waste."

"Ah. A pragmatist. I like that. What's your name?"

"Henry."

"No last name, Henry?"

"Not anymore."

"I see. A man running from his past. Is that what brought you to Epitaph?"

"No. I'm not afraid of the past."

He laughed, a hideous little laugh that made my skin crawl. "Then what are you afraid of, Henry?"

"The future."

"Well, let me put you at ease, my friend. You don't have a future. Nobody in Epitaph does."

"Why?"

"Because I'm going to kill every last one of you."

I nodded. "Yeah, I understood that. I meant why are you doing this? Killing a man is one thing. But this. This is something else altogether. Why are you doing it?"

"Would it be easier for you if I had a reason? Something you could comprehend?"

"No, but it might make it easier for you."

He thought about that for a moment and I could actually see a flicker of something in his eyes. Around us, most of the other men sat unmoving at their tables, as if they had been mesmerized in some way. All except a young farmer named Kabe, who was waving his hand at us.

The stranger saw my puzzled look and glanced back over his shoulder. Kabe stop waving and cleared his throat. "Something I can do for you, son?" the stranger asked.

Kabe pointed at his empty glass. "I'm just really scared, sir, and that makes me thirsty. Can I get some more whiskey?"

I thought the stranger was going to shoot him on the spot, but he seemed more amused than angry. "Help yourself, son, no need to go into the next life sober. Just stay away from the door."

I watched the young man as he dashed behind the bar, but the stranger turned his attention back to me.

"My dog died," he said.

"Pardon?" The oddness of the statement caught me completely off my guard.

"My dog died. I know it don't seem like much, but it was sort of the last straw, if you know what I mean." He took a deep breath as he turned things over in his mind. "A long time ago, I did some bad things."

"We all did."

"I'm not talking about the war. I used to be a terrible man. I took what I wanted and I killed anyone who tried to tell me otherwise. I had no regard for civilization."

I nodded, encouraging him. "What changed?"

"Everything. There was a woman, but it wasn't just her. At some point, something inside me turned and I decided I wanted a simpler life. Didn't want to be looking over my shoulder as I grew old. I spent some time in church. That's where I met her.

"Her father had just passed away, left her a piece of land, some crops. Turning farmer seemed like a good idea. So, I hung up my gun. We married and I started tending the crops. We had a son."

"I'm getting the idea that this doesn't end well."

"If it did, I wouldn't be here, would I?"

"I guess not."

"I wasn't much of a farmer. Never had the know-how. Crops eventually faltered. They didn't fail altogether, mind, they just weren't producing enough. Made it tough. Boy got hurt when he was ten. Fell off a horse. Wasn't nothing they could do for him."

"I'm sorry."

"Yeah, I heard that a lot. Wife couldn't handle the loss. Took to drink. A couple years went by and one morning she just didn't wake up. Then it was just me and the dog. You going to say sorry again?"

"Wasn't planning on it."

"Good. Hate that fucking word. Anyway, I was still trying. The gun was still hanging in the closet. I had lost damn near everything, but it seemed I still favored living a good life. And I still had that dog. He was a good dog, made my life bearable. That dog loved me like I was the greatest man that ever walked the earth."

"What happened?"

"Coyotes. I couldn't help him; my gun was still hanging in the closet. Hadn't worn it for almost twenty years. They tore him to pieces."

"That's a shame. I can see how that might be the last straw for a man. I can even see how you might want to take your own life. Just not sure I understand where killing everyone else comes into play."

"Way I see it, I made myself a deal with God all them years ago. I'd go straight, lead a good life, and he'd provide for me and mine. Make it a life worth living. That was his side of the deal, what he was paying me to cease my life of violence and mayhem. Well, he didn't live up to his side of the deal."

"So, you're making up for lost time? Causing all the destruction that would have been, had you not made your deal with Him?"

"It's a little bit more complicated than that in my head, but that's about the size of it."

"You realize that you're insane?"

He shook his head. "I think we're about done here, Henry." His eyes turned dark and his hand twitched just a little over the butt of his gun.

When you've been to war, or you've led a life of violence, you learn to recognize the important moments. The moments that keep you alive. It has nothing to do with bravery or heroism. It's entirely a thing of opportunity. A moment seized.

Kabe must have been listening intently to our conversation and the note of finality in the stranger's voice must have been more than his nerves could handle. The bottle he had been pouring from slipped from his fingers and shattered on the wooden floor.

It was just enough. The stranger couldn't help himself. His head snapped around toward the offending noise.

I seized the moment.

In a single motion I snapped my pistol from the table and fired, hitting him high in the back, penetrating his right shoulder. The impact spun him around and he was once again facing me, a look of profound disbelief upon his face. He drew his gun like lightning, but before he could fire, I shot him again, square in the chest.

Blood burst from his back like a fountain as he hung there for a brief piece of eternity, then he collapsed to the floor.

I stood up from my chair and walked over to his body, kicking the gun away from his hand. He laughed again, that horrible laugh, now punctuated with a horrible pain.

"You don't look happy, Henry," he gasped. "You should. You beat the devil."

"I made a promise, after the war, never to take another human life."

"Human? Do I still look human to you? I'm a monster, Henry."

"No. You're just a man." I pointed my Colt one final time and blew a hole right between his eyes. Then I lay my gun on the table and walked out of that saloon. Outside, in the distance, I could hear a coyote howl.

I took a deep breath and began walking out of Epitaph.

Sorry About The Money

Look, I'm really sorry about the money.

I meant to put it back. Really, I did. It's just, well, you know.

There was this girl, woman really, not girl. I suppose girl is sexist. Anyway, there was this woman. And I wanted to take her out. So, I just took a little from the register.

Borrowed. I meant to say borrowed, not took. I borrowed a little from the register. And I took her to this Chinese place, you know?

But she didn't like Chinese. I thought it was a safe choice. I mean, how was I supposed to know that she didn't like Chinese?

So, I took a little more from the register. Borrowed, I mean. Borrowed a little more. And I took her dancing. Nice club, upscale, live music. I thought she'd get into it.

She didn't like the band.

What do you do, you know? I thought she'd have a good time. It didn't work that way. So I asked her, what would you like to do? I asked her.

She starts talking about this little bed and breakfast upstate, and how much she liked it and the cozy fire and the big comfortable bed and she'd really like me to take her up there.

So, I borrowed some more from the register. I meant to put it back. Really, I did. But she was just incredible, and we had such a great time and…

I didn't know she was your wife.

I'm sorry.

Please don't kill me.

Neither Wind Nor Thunder With The Rain

No one could explain to Cleveland Harris why it was always raining. When they put the dome up, about five years ago, the engineers said it would be able to control the weather, not just protect them from the UV rays that were leaking through the remains of the ozone layer.

That was before some strange combination of the moisture in the soil, the water in the bay and the heating and cooling systems that crisscrossed the entire dome produced an unforeseen side effect: constant, drizzling rain. Committees were formed, studies were commissioned and budgets were examined. The result was predictable.

Nothing could be done. Since there were no actual storms, it was deemed an irritant, not a problem and the cost of redoing the heating grid would bankrupt the city and since there were no more federal funds to draw on, well, that was that. The net effect of this, also predictable, was that everyone wore raincoats, everyone wore hats and everyone walked around pissed off and miserable most of the time.

Which made them not only more likely to kill each other, but harder to identify because they all looked alike. A situation that made Harris even more miserable than the rest of them, because he was a detective for the city's homicide division and it was his job to sort it all out when people did knock each other off.

"At least this one's indoors," he muttered, as he climbed from his car and started for the old office building on Saratoga. Squad cars already surrounded the building, their lights flashing red and blue on the dimly lit street. Harris wore his badge on a chain around his neck, but no one would have stopped him anyway, they all knew the detective. Tall and broad, he was an imposing figure and at just over thirty his hair was completely white.

The crime scene itself was even more dismal and dreary than the street outside. At one time the ground floor of the office building had housed an upscale gym, but now it was just a large, gutted space. The electricity had been shut off long ago and the room was lit by several portable lanterns brought in by the crime lab. In the center of the former gym, amidst the trash and clutter left behind by years of homeless derelicts, was a body, dressed in black, lying face down on the floor.

"What have we got, Ben?" Harris asked.

"Two small caliber gunshot wounds to the back of the head," the crime lab tech answered. "Execution style."

Harris stared down at the corpse. "M.E. been here yet?"

"Still waiting."

"So, we can't move the body. Any evidence around?"

Ben Stafford grinned. "Tons. Probably all meaningless. This place hasn't been cleaned in twenty years and it looks like a favorite stopover spot for vagrants."

"Which will give us a whole flood of latent prints, all worthless. Terrific."

"Also, very little blood, so the guy probably wasn't killed here, just dumped."

Harris nodded, still looking at the body. Blonde, average build, average height. The M.E. would be more precise when he got him back to the morgue. Dressed in black, head to toe. "He's not wet."

The lab tech nodded. "Noticed that, huh? No coat, either. My people are looking for one, but I don't think they'll have any luck."

Harris kneeled down to get a closer look. Something caught his eye and he got down even closer, peering under the victim's chin. "Take a look at this."

Ben bent down and shined a pen light under the body. "Huh."

"What is that?"

"Looks like a priest's collar."

"A priest?" Harris asked.

"Yep. I didn't think there were any priests left in the city."

"There's not supposed to be. The Archdiocese pulled them out years ago. Claimed we had turned into a modern-day Gomorrah. Turns out it was really about the taxes the city started leveling on the church's land holdings."

"So, what's a priest doing here?"

Harris grunted. "Damned if I know." His scowl deepened as he stared at the body. This was starting to look like a mystery and Harris hated mysteries. He preferred clean cut, easy to close cases that wouldn't keep him awake at night. Harris was the type of cop that let little details nag at him if they didn't make sense. Little details that didn't stop nagging until he had a satisfactory answer for them.

Little details like what a priest was doing in his city.

"Who was first on the scene?"

"Dillon. He's taping the scene off out front."

Harris trudged outside, looked around, and spotted Pete Dillon leaning up against the fender of an old Ford. "How ya doing, Pete?"

"Not bad. Where's your partner?"

"Court. How'd you find the body?" Straight to business, Harris didn't much like Dillon and he didn't want to prolong the conversation.

"Anonymous call in. Said there'd be something interesting for us here."

"Something interesting? Those exact words?"

Dillon grinned. "Close enough. Weird, huh? The call was to 911, so it'll be on tape downtown, you can take a listen yourself."

Harris nodded. "What happened when you got here?"

"Pulled in about 2:15. Did a quick check of the outside perimeter, put on some gloves and went inside. Took a few steps, saw the body, stepped back out and called it in."

"Anybody nearby, any potential witnesses?"

"Not when I arrived. There were already a few milling around when I came back out, though. Probably saw the car, wondered what was up."

Harris looked up the street, then down the other direction. Nothing but rotted out stores, offices and warehouses. Nothing residential. "All right," he said, "round up some more uniforms. Work in teams, take flashlights, start poking around in all these closed stores, look for fresh puddles. Question anybody you find; these places are probably full of homeless people. See if anybody heard or saw anything. Anybody's story sounds odd, haul them downtown, we'll talk to them there."

Dillon stopped grinning. "That'll take all fucking night."

"Then you better get started."

Without waiting for an answer, Harris turned away and walked back to his own car. He reached through the open window, grabbed the radio handset and switched it on. "Dispatch, come in."

"Dispatch."

"This is detective Harris, badge 784395, working a homicide on Saratoga."

"What can I do for you, detective?"

"Pete Dillon caught the call on a 911 dispatch. I need to hear the tape of that call."

"One minute."

Harris leaned against the car while he waited and watched the chaos across the street. Dillon was trying to organize the other officers into teams, but no one seemed to be paying any attention to him. Harris smiled and was about to shout over some encouragement when dispatch finally came back on the line.

"I've got your call cued, detective. Should I play it now?"

"Go ahead."

There was an audible click, then a brief pause followed by "911, state the nature of your emergency."

A gravelly male voice responded, "I have a message for the police department."

"Is this an emergency, sir?"

"Not anymore. Just send a unit down to the old health club at the corner of Saratoga and Grand. They'll find something of interest inside." There was the sound of a phone hanging up and a moment later the recording clicked off. The voice seemed familiar to Harris.

"Is that what you needed, detective?" asked dispatch.

"Yeah. Now I need you to burn that to a couple of discs. Messenger one to me at the 38th Precinct, send the other one to voice analysis."

"Yes, sir."

Harris put the handset down and frowned. He hated mysteries.

Neil Merchant hated court.

It wasn't the testifying. He'd been a cop so long that testifying had become simple. Nice, relaxing, just the facts, no problems. It was the sitting around waiting to testify that pissed him off. Long wooden benches that made his ass hurt. Unpleasant people waiting alongside him for their chance to testify. Most of them were nervous, many of them smelled bad.

He hated people who smelled bad.

So, he was already in a foul mood before the judge dismissed the case. Illegal entry, no probable cause, all evidence deemed fruit of the poisoned tree. It made him scowl and the scowl made his youthful face look cracked and old.

By the time he got back to the precinct, his scowl had deepened and he was beginning to analyze the situation. Unlike his partner, Merchant actually liked mysteries and he thought he could see the corner of one sticking out from under the crushed remains of his case.

Harris was already back at his desk, diligently typing up the initial report on the priest's murder, a task made all the more difficult for Harris because he could only type with two fingers.

"Hey, Cleve," Merchant said. "What have we got?"

"Dead priest in an abandoned building," he muttered without looking up. "How'd court go?"

Merchant dropped into his chair. "Lousy. Judge threw out the case."

That got Harris' attention. "Threw it out? What for?"

"Said we didn't have probable cause."

"What about the scream?"

Two weeks earlier, Harris and Merchant had gone to an apartment building on Bleeker Street to question one Devon Mulrooney about his possible involvement in selling a .45 caliber handgun to a gentleman who had used said gun to kill his boss. Before knocking, they heard a scream from inside the apartment, drew their guns and kicked in the door. Turns out Mulrooney was alone inside, but the vidserver volume was maxed out and they figured the scream must have come from there. Inside, in plain sight, were nearly a hundred guns in various shapes and sizes, so they arrested Mulrooney for illegal possession of firearms.

"The defense said there was no scream on the vidserver. They did their research, Cleve. They went to every damn channel and verified what they were running at that time. Nobody was airing anything that had someone screaming, not even during a commercial."

Harris stared at him blankly. "We heard a scream. Both of us heard it, plain as day."

"Yeah, I know. I've been thinking about that."

"Shit."

"Yeah."

"We missed something. Someone else in the building in trouble, maybe. Sound came from another apartment."

"Seems like the most likely explanation."

"We have to go back, don't we?"

"Yeah."

"Shit." Harris stood up, clipped on his gun and slipped into his coat. "May as well get it over with, I'm still waiting on an M.E. report and voice analysis."

"Voice analysis?"

"Yeah, come on, I'll fill you in on the way."

The apartment building on Bleeker Street was a slum, of course. Old, dilapidated, filthy and it smelled of urine and cigarettes. Harris and Merchant moved carefully up the steps until they reached the third-floor landing, where Mulrooney lived. They stood in front of his door and frowned.

"Does it ever bother you that all these places look alike?" Harris asked.

"What do you mean?"

"Never mind. So, where do we start?"

"Not a clue." Merchant looked up and down the hall. "Could have come from the next floor up, I suppose. Or the one below."

"What do we do, knock on their doors and say, 'hey, did you happen to scream really loud on the 14th, about 8:30 at night?"

Merchant shook his head. "No, I guess not. I don't suppose we could get a warrant to search the whole building."

"Hey, you guys! You here about the smell?"

They both turned and looked down the hall in the direction of the shout. It was a scruffy looking old man, gray of hair and beard, dressed in a pair of dirty old long johns.

"Excuse me?" Merchant said.

"The smell! The smell! What are you, God damned deaf? Are you here about the smell?"

Before Merchant could say anything, Harris interrupted. "Yeah, we're here about the smell, but dispatch didn't give us the apartment number of the complainant. We were just trying to decide how to proceed."

The old man got more agitated. "Well, I'm the God damned complainer, I guess, and you can start by getting rid of that smell."

They walked down the hall and joined the old man at his apartment. "Where's it coming from?" Merchant asked.

"How the hell should I know, you're the damned experts. Come inside and smell for your damn selves."

They entered the old man's apartment and stopped in their tracks. They had both been cops long enough that they instantly recognized the smell of death. "Where's it coming from?" Merchant asked again, but this time the question was directed at Harris. The old man started to say something, but saw the seriousness of their expressions and opted against it.

"It's not in here," Harris answered. "It's distinct, but not strong enough. Through the ventilation system?" He walked over to the air vents in the wall and sure enough, the smell was stronger. He pulled a Swiss army knife from his pocket and undid the screws on the vent cover.

"Well?" Merchant asked.

Harris stuck his face into the vent and sniffed up and down. "Upstairs, I think. Hard to be sure."

Out the door they went, leaving the confused old man behind and hurried up the steps to the next landing. Finding the apartment above the old man's, which happened to be just above and to the right of Mulrooney's place, they stood outside the door. The odor was stronger up here. With a vague sense of déjà vu, they unholstered their guns and kicked the door in unison. It flew open and the smell was suddenly over whelming.

Holding his breath, Merchant peered inside.

There was blood everywhere.

And in the center of the living room, exactly what they knew would be there.

A body.

For the second time that day, Harris was sitting around waiting for the M.E.

After they had called it in, Merchant and Harris had done a quick once over of the apartment. The tenant, a young woman, probably in her mid-twenties, had been stabbed repeatedly. The knife was left lying on the floor near the body and of course the whole place was drenched in blood.

They found no identification in the apartment, nothing to indicate who she might be. Harris asked dispatch to try to reach the landlord, find out whose name was on the lease.

"In the old days," Merchant said, "the forensic boys would have been all over this place, telling us everything we needed to know about the perp."

"Yeah, but in the old days we actually had a budget. We're lucky to get a single real lab guy down here to process the room and then it's only a once over."

"Think there'll be any DNA?"

"That we can use?" Harris muttered. "Maybe, maybe not. If they can get something off the body, maybe under the nails or something, if she fought back, then we might have a shot. Not the room in general, though, probably been too many people in here over the years and it doesn't look like she was much of a housekeeper."

The lab guy came and went without saying much, so Harris had no idea if he was going to get anything useful from that. Merchant was off questioning tenants in the rest of the building on the off chance that someone might have seen or heard something. Unfortunately, at the same time the young woman was being murdered, they were busting down Mulrooney's door and anyone likely to be paying attention to the comings and goings in the building was probably distracted by the action on the third floor.

Hell, the killer could have walked right by them that night and no one would have noticed. Except...

"There's a convenience store across the street," Harris muttered. He stuck his head in the room and told the uniform guarding the scene that he'd be right back if anyone asked, then took off down the steps and out the front door.

The clerk at the store looked at him blankly when he flashed his badge. He was a young guy, maybe eighteen, with no hair, a lot of tattoos and some basic body mods, horns and a ridge down the center of his skull.

"I don't know what you want, Mr. Suit, and I don't give a shit. I'm over here minding my own bidness, ain't got nothing to do wit you."

"Uh-huh." Harris considered his choices for a moment, weighing tact and discretion against brute force and anger. Maybe a blend of the two. He leaned on the counter and smiled. "Listen, you little shit, I don't have the patience to play games with you." His voice was calm and measured but his eyes told a very different story. "A woman over in that building is dead. She died two weeks ago, on the fourteenth, between eight and nine pm. Now, you have a security camera here that points at your front door. See it? It should also see that door across the street because the line of sight is perfect through this glass door. So, I want the discs from the fourteenth or I'm going to rip those horns right off your fucking head. Are we clear?"

The young man stammered and stuttered for a minute, but he went to the back and pulled the discs and that was all that mattered. Harris took them from him and went down to his car to grab the netpad from the trunk. Just as he sat down on the curb, Merchant came out looking for him.

"Hey, there you are."

Harris nodded. "How'd it go inside?'

"About what we expected. Not a damn thing. M.E. finally got here, he's inside now. What've you got?"

"Discs from the security camera across the street. Let's see if we got lucky." Harris was often lucky. It was something he had begun to rely on, probably more than he should.

The terminal allowed them to zoom through the glass door and focus on the front door of the apartment building. The problem was, when they were going into the building, people had their backs to the camera. They couldn't identify anyone but themselves when they entered around 8:30. Shortly after that the traffic increased, becoming almost a mob of people going in and out of the house.

"We're going to have to get this to the lab and see if they can get printouts of each face coming out of the building. At least the ones that aren't shrouded by their damn hats. Then we can compare them against the people who should be there and see if we end up with any strangers."

Merchant was looking at the screen, absorbing everything. "Wait a minute, Cleve, back it up a few frames."

Harris rolled the image back. "What did you see?"

"The guy on the far right coming down the stairs, is he wearing what I think he's wearing?"

Harris looked at the image again.

"Shit. How did I miss that? That's him."

He brought the image in tighter on the man's face.

And on the white priest's collar around his neck.

Two hours later Harris and Merchant were sitting in an empty interrogation chamber, sorting through the reports on both cases. The medical reports had started filtering in on the priest, but the details weren't very helpful so far. Tox screens had turned up a heavy concentration of barbiturates in his system along with some alcohol. Not enough to kill him, but he wouldn't be very active, either.

They found nothing in the city print or DNA databanks to match him and they probably couldn't get approval to do a national search, not a high enough profile case, the chief would never authorize the expense. Besides nobody ever came to the city. It wasn't exactly a tourist attraction. The autopsy confirmed that cause of death was two gunshots to the back of the head. Recovered bullet fragments showed the gun to be of a .380 caliber.

There was no identification or personal effects on the body. A canvas of the neighborhood turned up exactly what Harris expected to turn up. Nothing. Nobody had seen anything suspicious; nobody had seen a priest or anyone else near the old health club. He had uniforms questioning the neighbors at Bleeker Street armed with photographs of the priest, but that would take time.

Merchant stared at one of the photographs for a minute and asked, "Can we place him in the girl's apartment?"

Harris shrugged. "Who knows? Deitrich pulled seventy some separate prints from that place and it's going to take a while to process them. If we're lucky, we'll put the priest inside. Then what?"

Merchant shuffled through some papers. "Landlord said the place was rented out to a Derek Roth. No mention of a wife or girlfriend living there."

"And no sign of a man living there when we went through the apartment. Only her things in the closets. Only one toothbrush in the bathroom. You think this Derek Roth is the priest?"

"It's possible. Let me run him through the computer, we got a social security number on the lease." Merchant switched on the wireless terminal and typed the number into the city databank. A few seconds later he had an answer. "Zip. No one using that number has ever been arrested or employed in the city."

"Why am I not surprised? Everything about this case makes my head hurt."

"Want me to make it hurt more?" This came not from Merchant, but from the doorway. They both turned to see Sam Kreiger, the aging tech from the video analysis section. He stood in the doorway, broad as a wall and hairy as a bear, not a trace of gray even though department rumors put him at almost seventy years old.

Harris just frowned, but Merchant took the bait. "What have you got, Sam?"

Kreiger strode into the room and laid a bunch of photos down on the table. They were still images of the priest coming out of the apartment building with the rest of the crowd. "Okay, take a close look at his nose."

"His nose?" Harris asked.

"Yeah, his nose. Notice anything?"

"Looks like a normal nose to me," Merchant muttered.

"There's a shadow along the right-hand side of it, which would place the light source to the left. Now look at everyone else's noses."

"Shadows are on the other side," Harris said.

"Score."

"How it that possible?"

Kreiger grinned. "It's not. These images have been doctored. That man shouldn't be there. It's an extraordinary job, I'll give you that. No pixelization, seamless edging. And this was in full motion video, not just still images. Very impressive."

Harris and Merchant looked at each other, then back at Krieger.

"That film came from a security camera at a convenience store. Who would mess with a security camera?"

The old man's grin widened as he headed for the door. "Not my problem boys, you're the detectives."

They sat at the table, flipping back and forth through the photos. After a few minutes, Merchant said, "Why didn't we notice that?"

"Cause it's a fucking security camera. When's the last time you had a doctored security cam disc? I'll tell you when. Fucking never, that's when." Harris stood up and started pacing the room. "It doesn't make any damn sense, Neil. We got a dead priest who shouldn't even be in the city, we can't identify him, he shows up in the security footage on a completely unrelated case and now the footage is doctored."

Merchant watched as his partner paced about the room. Harris' behavior at times like these always fascinated him. He knew Harris hated mysteries, but he was actually very good at solving them, much better than Merchant himself would ever be. Right before a breakthrough he would start pacing like this, muttering to himself, then he'd pull a plan out of thin air and it almost always led them in the right direction. Merchant considered himself very lucky to be partnered up with Cleveland Harris.

Almost as suddenly as it started, the pacing stopped. Harris crossed to the phone and dialed the number for the morgue. He said something about coming down to see the priest's body, then scowled as he listed to the reply. "How," he asked and then listened some more. The expression on his face grew darker and darker and he hurled the phone across the room.

Almost afraid to ask, Merchant stood up and said, "What is it, Cleve?"

"The priest's body, it's gone."

Harris didn't sleep that night. He spent his time walking the streets, listening to the cold, still rain and thinking.

He never slept when he had a case like this, where things didn't fit together logically. He'd turn them over and over in his mind and try to make the pieces fit together.

There was obviously something big he wasn't seeing. The problem was he just didn't know anything, yet. He didn't even know who the victims were, so how could he possibly tie them together? Maybe some more information would filter in from the apartment murder. Maybe the girl's prints would be in the databanks.

By morning, he had run through every piece of evidence he had hundreds of times and was still drawing a blank. He gave up on the idea of sleep and headed back to the precinct. Maybe some of the reports had come in overnight.

The squad room was quiet.

Merchant wasn't due for another two hours. Neither were the rest of the day shift detectives. The night shift guys were probably out at a crime scene. Only the log officer was at his desk and he seemed almost asleep.

Harris sat down at his desk and reached for the case folder for the priest. He paused. It was labeled now, with a name. Martin Holloway. Had they identified the priest while he was out? Why hadn't someone called him?

He looked at the outside of the folder and for some reason, it made him nervous. He didn't want to open it.

He looked at the name written in the black marker, neat and precise. It looked like his own writing. Hands unsteady, he flipped open the cover. Inside were crime scene photos, but not the ones that had been there before. He closed the cover and looked at the address again. It was the right file, the old gym.

The photos showed the same scene, but the body was different. This man was blonde and dressed in light colored clothing. He flipped through the reports. All the same, except there was no mention of the priest's collar. And his fingerprints had been on file, that's how a positive ID had been made.

Harris scowled at the reports.

They all had his signature on them. Even the fingerprint search request.

He picked up the phone and dialed the forensics lab. "Is Stafford in yet?" he asked. They put him on hold. He sat there, stomach reeling, unable to comprehend. When the lab tech finally came on the phone, he could hardly speak. "That case we caught yesterday," he mumbled, "on Saratoga Street?"

"At the old gym, yeah, what about it?"

"Do you remember what he was wearing?"

Stafford paused. "Don't you have pictures, Cleve?"

"Humor me, tell me what he was wearing."

"Okay. Khaki pants, pale blue oxford, dark brown shoes. He didn't have a coat and he wasn't wet, is that what you're looking for?"

"You remember anything about a collar?"

"His collar? Normal collar for an Oxford, why?"

"Never mind." Harris hung up the phone and leaned back in his chair. A joke? It seemed impossible. Could he be losing it, could the whole thing have been in his mind? He didn't think so, but would he know if he was going crazy?

He sat there, just thinking it through, until Merchant arrived.

"Solve the case yet, Cleve?" he asked.

Harris just stared at him.

After a minute, Merchant said, "something wrong?"

"Just wondering if you're in on it."

"Huh?"

Harris shook his head. "Nothing, never mind. Do you remember that priest yesterday?"

"Priest?" Merchant shook his head. "No, I don't remember any priest. We don't have priests in the city anymore, do we?"

"No, I guess we don't." He stood up and started for the exit.

"Hey, Cleve, where ya going?"

"To get my head examined," Harris muttered and walked out the door.

Harris thought it was a joke at the time.

But after a visit to both crime scenes, he found himself more confused than ever, so he headed for the department's medical infirmary. It took some doing to convince the doctors to run tests on him without an explanation why, but eventually they agreed.

They did a basic physical exam, took x-rays and ran an EEG test. They all came back fine. As a final check they ran a Brainwave Sensory Impulse test. That wasn't fine.

Harris was pacing the examination room when Dr. Phillips came back with the results. "Well," he asked. "What is it?"

The doctor shook his head. "I don't know. Let me show you something." He spread out a long piece of paper that showed numerous lines in various colors, crisscrossing in intricate patterns. "These represent the various electrical impulses in your brain. We're still learning what all of them do. It's not an exact science, yet, by any means. However, we do know one thing. Do you see this gray line here?

"Yes."

"You shouldn't. I've never seen it on another BSI test. Ever. There should be thirty-two separate and distinct lines. You have thirty-three."

"What does that mean?"

Dr. Phillips frowned. "I'm not sure how to answer that. Like I said, I've never seen anything like it before. I pulled your file and compared it to your old test, that one was normal. So, whatever happened to you, happened since your last mandatory physical evaluation. That would lead me to believe that it's artificial, rather than some sort of natural mutation."

"Artificial? As in someone fucking with my brain?"

"That would be my first thought, yes, but it brings up another question that I can't answer. How? I did a careful examination of your skull, there's no recent wounds of any kind, no injection marks. Your toxicology report shows no foreign chemicals in your bloodstream. It's a physiological change, so it can't be accounted for by something like hypnotism. I just don't know how it could have been done."

Harris thought about it for a minute. "Could this affect my memory? Or cause hallucinations?"

"There's no real way to tell. Have you been having problems with either?"

"Well..."

"I can't help you if you don't tell me."

"Shit. You're right." Harris resumed his pacing as he went back over the previous day's events with the doctor, step by step. When he was finished, he sat down on the examination table and waited while the doctor thought it over.

"So, if it was an altered reality, it's been corrected today. You haven't seen the priest at all today, just things as they really should be, correct?"

"Yeah, I guess so. I can't find any reference to the priest in anything, even my own reports."

"Detective, I hate to say this, but that presents a new problem."

Harris grimaced. "Why doesn't that surprise me? Okay, doc, unload. What is it?"

"Well, if your mind was tampered with yesterday, somehow, then it could have added that thirty-third wave to the BSI test. But if the alteration was undone, the wave shouldn't still be there. So, there's the possibility that what you're experiencing today is the alteration."

"But…" He sat silent for a minute then said, "What about everybody else? They don't remember the priest at all."

"Two possibilities. Either your perceptions of what they tell you are being altered or their memories of yesterday are altered as well."

"Then why would I have memories of the priest, when they don't?"

"You said you didn't sleep last night; you were too caught up in the case. Maybe you need to be inactive for the change to take effect."

"So, when I do get to sleep, I could forget everything about the priest?"

"Yes, It's possible. Probable, even."

Harris considered it for a moment. "All right, doc, I'm going to try to get my partner to come in for a BSI test. Don't explain anything to him, just run the test. I need to know if others are really being affected by this."

"Okay, I can do that."

"In the meantime, I think you better give me some stim packs. I can't afford to sleep until I figure this mess out."

As Harris left the med building and started down the large, ornate steps, he stopped dead in his tracks. Across the street, on a bench in front of the park, sat the priest, reading a newspaper. He made his way down the rest of the steps and across the street without taking his eyes from his quarry.

Two steps away, he stopped and said, "You're under arrest."

"For what, detective? With what crime can you possible charge me? Being alive?" His voice had a strange lilt to it, almost European, but not quite.

"Tampering with evidence. Interfering with a murder investigation."

"Really?" The priest neatly folded the paper and laid it on the bench beside him. "And how do you expect to make that stick, detective? Nobody else even believes I exist."

"The doctor?"

"Being taken care of as we speak. An oversight on my part, I never expected you to go that route. But then, that's what these things are all about, isn't it? The unpredictability?"

Harris stared at him and frowned. "You ever have one of those days where you feel really dense? Like the answers are all in front of you and you just can't see them clearly?"

"Happens to the best of us, detective." There was a slight tinge of sarcasm every time the priest used the word 'detective'.

"You know what's going on, don't you?"

"Do you have any siblings, detective?"

Harris thought about it. "That's weird. I can't remember."

"Of course, you can't."

"Who are you?"

The priest smiled. "You can call me Gary, how's that?"

"Father Gary?"

"If you like, yes. In fact, I rather like that."

"What are you after, Father? What do you want?"

"Inconsistency. Mistakes. I want you to see the flaws in the design. Like the newspaper lying at my side. You can't quite read it, can you? Even though the banner is right on top, it's just out of focus."

Harris shook his head. "The words are English, but I don't understand a damn thing you say."

"I think you do, son. Deep down inside, I think I'm starting to get through. The puzzle isn't making sense anymore, you keep turning it over and over and it doesn't make any sense at all. You can keep twisting it, trying to fit the facts into your preconceived notions or you can step back and look at the larger picture. Think outside the box, as they used to say in those silly TV ads."

The scowl of Harris' face deepened. "There's a pattern here and I'll find it. And I'll nail you with it."

"Such hostility. Tell me detective, what is your mother's maiden name? Was she a good cook? Could she make an apple pie? You can't remember, can you? Do you feel a slight itching sensation on the back of your head? Down at the base of your neck? I can tell you why. I can even make it go away, if you let me."

Unconsciously, Harris began to scratch at his neck.

"Don't let him fool you, Cleve." It was Merchant, suddenly standing there, as if he'd been there all along. His gun was drawn and aimed at the priest.

Father Gary smiled. "Now there's a development I didn't expect."

Harris looked back and forth between them. Merchant looked frightened, but the priest did not. An odd reversal, considering their positions.

"I don't think he's armed, Neil," Harris said.

"He's already killed two officers, Cleve."

The priest stopped smiling. "Oh my. It's not only gained some form of sentience; it's writing its own scenario. That shouldn't be possible. Although it does explain a few things. His consciousness was probably fighting with yours, each filling in details of an impossible crime."

Harris looked even more confused. Ideas were starting to break through, but he could feel his mind pushing them away. He looked at Merchant and frowned. "He hasn't killed anyone, Neil. He's the vic, remember?"

"The vic? What's wrong with you, Cleve? He's standing right there. He's not dead.

"No," said Father Gary. "I'm not, am I?"

Then Harris started to hear voices.

They were faint at first, but then they started to get just a little louder. They seemed to come from nowhere and everywhere at once and they were directed at the priest.

"I don't understand why you don't just pull the plug," one of the voices muttered. It sounded familiar, but he couldn't place it.

"Too dangerous," answered another voice, one that sounded like the 911 dispatch officer. "He has to do it himself."

"It's leaking in, isn't it?" The priest asked.

"What's leaking in?"

"Reality."

Harris turned from him and started to walk away. Away from the priest and from his partner. I'll go back to my apartment, he decided. I'll lie down a bit, think things through. It would all fall into place. It always did.

He walked several blocks down to First Avenue and stopped. Which way was his home? He knew it was off First Avenue, but what direction? Why didn't he know?

"You don't know where your apartment is, do you? You've never had a reason to know." It was the priest again, right behind him. "The action of the story never necessitated it."

"Don't listen to him, Cleve." His partner was there, too, behind the priest. "He's trying to confuse you."

Harris ignored him and focused on Father Gary. "The story?" He tried to regain his composure so he could think. "You're not really a priest, are you?"

"No, I'm not."

"Then why the get up?"

"You're a lapsed catholic, Cleveland. This is the face you assign to authority that you don't understand."

"I assign. Like I gave you that appearance?"

"Precisely."

"Your name isn't really Gary, is it?"

"No, it's not."

Harris sat down on the curb, feeling defeated. Merchant was gone now and the street seemed different, out of focus. "So why do I call you that?" he asked.

"Another clue from your sub-conscious, I believe."

"From my…" His voice trailed off as he thought about it. "Gary Gygax," he whispered. "Of course." The pieces finally started to fall into place. "How long have I been in here?" he asked.

"Four weeks."

"Wow. Where was the scenario supposed to end?"

"With the Mulrooney case. But you got too caught up in the program and just kept right on playing."

"Unjack me."

The world seemed to implode around him, the city shrunk away into his eyes and became a blinding white light that gradually faded into the slightly dimmer light of a science lab. He tried to sit up from the fitted bed he rested in, but his muscles wouldn't cooperate.

"Don't try to push it, Cleve, you've been there for weeks." The voice was that of the priest from the scenario, but the face belonged to Professor Daniel Hampton, the inventor of the virtual gaming system that had been his prison.

"My head hurts like hell."

"That plug is designed for two weeks, maximum. You doubled that time. I was afraid you were never going to come out. What finally got through to you?"

"Father Gary, Gary Gygax, father of the role-playing game. Once that clicked it all came together. I think the game needs a few more safeguards before you put it on the market, Professor."

Hampton shook his head in agreement. "I know, I know. I'm already working on it. What about texturally? Anything it lacks?"

"Wind. Thunder and wind. If you're going to have that much rain, you've got to have thunder and wind."

Stuck in a Cupboard With You

The Great Detective was locked in a cupboard.

It wouldn't have been quite so embarrassing if it had happened in the course of an investigation, while he was searching for some vital clue that would unravel a complex mystery and allow him to once again save the day.

Instead, it had happened after a few too many brandies, and a few too many "Did I ever tell you about the time Holmes and I…?" stories from Watson. He had left the parlor of their host in search of a washroom, and had turned left instead of right, and the next thing he knew, there he was amidst the linen, which he had to admit was quite comfortable.

He had only agreed to come to the wretched dinner party because he had heard that Irene Adler was back in London after all these years, to perform at a musical gala being sponsored by the host of this wretched dinner party (a phrase which he felt being seared into his memory), and he had hoped that she might put in an appearance at this wretched dinner party (The Adventure of the Wretched Dinner Party, as Watson might put it).

Not for any of the ridiculous romantic reasons that Watson hinted at in his oddly passive-aggressive musings, but simply to do her the public courtesy of acknowledging her as his intellectual equal. Of course, that was off the table now. You can't possibly refer to your towering intellect after being locked in a cupboard for the better part of an hour.

She was there now (of course she was), he had heard her voice shortly after he had heard the maid latch the cupboard door, while making a tetch, tetch noise at her falsely perceived forgetfulness.

The timing of that moment was remarkable. He had stumbled in, bumped his knee of a shelf, realized that it was both dark and not the washroom, turned to exit, heard Irene's voice ("Doctor Watson, so nice to finally meet you...") and almost simultaneously, heard the tetch, tetch and the click as the latch snapped into place.

He could have, at that very moment, simply had said something, anything, and the maid would have heard him and let him out. But his ego held his tongue and the moment passed. He listened as the maid walked away, sighed, and began thinking of ways to get out of the cupboard on his own.

Forty-five minutes later, he sat, thinking about how remarkably effective a simple door latch could be. His agile mind had worked through over seventy different ways of getting out of his predicament, but unfortunately, none of them managed to do the trick with his dignity intact. He had been listening to the conversation in the parlor, and it had evolved from the mundane ("Where is Mr. Holmes? He was just here, he'll be back in a moment.") to the ridiculous ("Perhaps he's been abducted. Should we send for Lestrade?") over the last thirty odd minutes.

Now, from what he had heard, Watson was out searching the estate grounds. It was getting worse by the moment, and he knew it. There was simply no alternative. He was going to have to shout for help. And then change his name and move out of the country.

He was about to raise his voice when he heard footsteps padding softly toward the cupboard. A hand fumbled with the latch and the door opened. Standing there, looking ever so slightly startled, was the beautiful Irene Adler.

"Oh," she said. "I was looking for the washroom."

"Yes, so was I," said Holmes.

"This isn't it."

"No, no it isn't."

"It looks comfortable, though."

"It is, rather."

Irene smiled and stepped into the cupboard. She sat next to Holmes and let the door close. "Yes, you're right, it is."

And then, inevitably, came the tetch, tetch noise, and the clicking of the latch. "Was that?" Irene asked.

"The door being latched shut? Yes, it was."

"Oh."

"Yes," said Holmes, although for some reason he was no longer concerned with getting out of the cupboard. In the distance, he could hear Watson calling his name, and beside him, Irene laughing ever so softly in his ear.

Dead at Five

"They're all on screen! Look! One, two, three, four. Who's operating the camera?"

"Julian," I said, "it's just a movie."

"That's not the point. Look at the box or the website. The producers are calling it a documentary. They say it's real and it's obviously not. Somebody should do something about this."

I suppose I could have sat and argued with him, but I didn't feel like it. Of course, I was married to the man, so I learned years ago not to add fuel to his rants. It just makes him worse. Ask Inspector Rodriguez at Homicide South. He's been stoking

Julian's fires for as long as I've known him and it always blows up in his face. Some people never learn.

I left Julian to his movie and strolled into the kitchen to fix a drink. It was a little early in the day, but we didn't have anything going on right now and even if someone turned up, it would have to be a pretty unusual case to get Julian away from the television. Ever since he bought the DVD player last month, followed by a new widescreen TV and a few hundred DVDs, he'd been glued to the set. I tried getting him to tackle a missing persons case last week, but he just referred the client to another agency downtown. He was too busy with the scene workshop on the *Men In Black* disc.

I was just throwing ice in the blender when the buzzer rang. We live in a penthouse apartment just off Park Avenue and the buzzer meant the doorman. I walked over to the intercom and clicked it on. "Yes?"

"Mrs. West? There's a Mr. and Mrs. Hovarth here to see Mr. West." I thought about it for a moment. There was always a chance that Julian would see them. Then again, he might toss them out without a second thought. Still....

I glanced down at myself. Jeans and t-shirt, not the best way to greet a prospective client. "Harry? Hold on to them for about 10 minutes, while I make things presentable. They don't have an appointment, so I'm sure they won't mind. Then go ahead and send them up."

"Yes, ma'am."

I dashed into the bedroom and changed into a simple skirt and blouse, pulled on some stockings and checked my hair in the mirror. Very professional, no make-up needed. I stepped into a pair of flats and was just walking into the living room when the front doorbell rang.

"Mr. and Mrs. Hovarth? How are you? I'm Melanie West." We exchanged pleasantries and I ushered them inside, using the time to size them up. Mid 30's, a pleasant looking couple, if you made allowances for the worried expressions on their faces. No one forced to call on a private detective is going to look like a bundle of joy.

It's hard to tell from clothing anymore, but most people still wear their tax bracket like a badge, the clues are just subtler. Usually I look at the shoes, the watch and the haircut. Even dressed in grunge clothes, most people don't bother to adjust those items down accordingly. From what I could gather from the Hovarths, I'd have guessed them at the lower middle-class level. Combined income, maybe in the sixties. That's not a judgment on them as people, it just didn't bode well for a flat fee, which meant it would have to be really good to get Julian involved.

I offered them refreshments, which they both turned down, then left them on a comfy couch in the living room while I headed for the den, excuse me, the home theater, to get my husband.

He was still watching The St. Francisville Experiment, even more agitated then before. He hit the pause button, looked up at me and scowled.

"I heard the door. The answer is no. Send them to Hasden on Houston Street. He needs the work."

"So do we. Have you looked at the checking account?"

"Not lately."

"You should. This little theater of yours has run close to ten thousand, counting all your damn movies. You know you can rent the things at Blockbuster, don't you? You don't have to buy one of each. Especially stuff you haven't seen before. You can't tell me this mockumentary was a good investment."

He looked down at his lap and stuck his lips out, like a pouting child. "It was only twenty dollars."

"Only twenty dollars adds up after several hundred movies. The way things stand now, you can forget about dinner at Valencia's on Friday. We'll be eating at McDonald's."

It was a tough call. If I dropped it there and left the room, he might be shamed enough to pull his act together and come meet the clients. Then again, he could continue to pout and go back to his movie, refusing to come out. I'd say it was fifty-fifty. I tossed a mental coin, saw George Washington's face in my mind, turned and walked back to the living room.

"Julian's just finishing up with a couple of reports, he'll be right out. Are you sure I can't get you something to drink?"

Mrs. Hovarth reaffirmed her original decision, but the Mr. recanted and asked for a glass of water. I was glad to have something to do, and headed for the kitchen wondering what I was going to say if Julian never emerged. I needn't have bothered. Just as I returned with Mr. Hovarth's water, Julian made his entrance.

I say it like that, because he always looks so theatrical to me when he enters a room. Of course, part of that is his classic, leading man looks, sort of a boyish Cary Grant. But it's not just that. He always insists on greeting a client in a nicely tailored suit and he has this trick of stopping in the doorway as he enters a room, seeking the eyes of the newcomers and then turning on his hundred-watt smile. Then he strides into the room, holding out his hand and saying...

"Hello. I'm Julian West."

Our prospective clients rose to greet him. "I'm Donald Hovarth, this is my wife, Linda."

Julian shook Donald's hand and gave Linda's an elegant kiss. "Please, make yourselves comfortable. Are you still working for Channel 8, Donald?"

The look on Hovarth's face was priceless. He fell back onto the couch and stared up at Julian with his mouth agape. His wife looked back and forth between them, obviously puzzled. "You know my husband?" she asked.

Julian grinned. "Just the name. Don't worry, Linda, it's nothing sordid or even amazing on my part. I have a photographic memory and I watch the credits on the evening news. Donald Hovarth is a cameraman for Channel 8. I just took a chance that you were the same Donald Hovarth and apparently, I hit the mark. What can I do for you?"

Hovarth's face relaxed a bit and he and his wife settled back on the couch. Julian sat in a chair across from them, and after giving Hovarth his glass of water, I took a chair at the end of the couch, by Linda.

There was an uncomfortable silence in the room for a few minutes as Hovarth worked through it in his mind, trying to find a starting place. Finally, he made up his mind and pulled a small bundle, wrapped in a scarf from his jacket pocket. It made a heavy thud as he sat it down on the coffee table.

"That's the long and short of the problem, Mr. West. There are details, of course. There always are. But that's the central issue."

Julian turned to me and raised an eyebrow. I shook my head. No idea. Carefully, he leaned forward and unwrapped the bundle. We both gave it a good look. Stainless steel, black handle, revolver, Smith & Wesson engraved on the barrel, .38.

"Melanie, could you get me a pencil and a handkerchief?"

I disappeared into the bedroom for a moment, but when I returned, they were still sitting in silence. I handed the pencil to Julian and he slid it through the trigger guard and lifted the revolver in the air, bringing it close to his face to smell the cylinder. Then he used the handkerchief to push the release and open it up.

"Four shells, two empty cartridges. Is this your gun, Donald?"

Hovarth frowned. "I don't know."

"I see. Well, that complicates matters. Do you have reason to suspect that this gun has been used in the commission of a crime? Think about it before you answer. As a licensed private detective in the state of New York, I have certain legal obligations. If I obtain evidence that a crime has been committed, and the police do not have that evidence, I am required by law to turn it over to them. I ask again, do you have reason to believe this weapon was used in the commission of a crime?"

"Not specifically, no."

"All right. Before I ask for any details, we should make this official. If I'm acting in your behalf, I have some leeway in what I have to turn over to the police. I can reasonably protect your interests unless it turns out that any crime committed was at your hand. I'll need a retainer."

Linda shuffled a bit and reached for her pocketbook. Apparently, talking money made her feel a little more at ease. "Will $500 be enough?"

I said yes. "As an advance against expenses. The fee will be determined by the work itself and the outcome of the case, as well as your ability to pay. Julian is usually expensive, but we don't gouge people."

After the check was entered in the ledger and a receipt was issued, we got back to business. "Why don't you start where it feels comfortable to you," Julian said, "and as I develop questions, I'll ask them."

Hovarth nodded his agreement, and after taking his wife's hand, he began. "I've had a rough year. Well, we've had a rough year, I should say. It started with the death of my sister. My parents had both passed away when we were young. We were raised by an aunt, so Cindy was the only close relative I had. I might have been able to handle it if it had been natural, if I had warning, who knows. But it didn't happen that way. She just fell in a bathtub, cracked her skull. She lived alone, so it was a week before anyone discovered the body.

"I couldn't deal with it. I just walked around like a zombie, doing everything in a paint by numbers kind of way. Linda took it okay for a while, but when I didn't show any signs of recovery, it started to wear on her. We stopped communicating. Not intentionally. I didn't refuse to speak to her. I just didn't seem to have anything to say. So, we drifted apart.

"And the reality of that made me worse. I started drinking heavily. Popping pills. Linda wanted me to go to a doctor, a therapist or something, but I wouldn't. Then I got worse. Almost catatonic. I had some kind of breakdown, whatever you want to call it. Linda started going through my things, flushing pills, afraid that I'd do something to hurt myself. That's when she found the gun. Wrapped up, just like that, in the back of my closet. A week later, I started to come out of it. To communicate again. In a couple of days, she asked me about it. I told her that I didn't remember it, that I had never owned a gun. I've never even fired one. We thought about going to the police, but with my recent condition, I realized that I could have done anything during my mental state."

"So, you came to me?"

"That was my idea," Linda said.

I got a notepad from the desk and sat back down. "May I ask a couple of questions?"

Julian leaned back in his chair and relaxed. This was a normal part of the routine. I'd nail down the details and he'd let his mind float around looking for things that didn't feel right.

"Mr. Hovarth, exactly when did your sister die?" I asked.

"May 12th, they think. It's a little vague, because her body was in the water. They said that it makes it difficult to pinpoint an exact day."

"They're right. We'll just say sometime around May 12th. That's about eleven months ago. I assume you took some time off before going back to work?"

"A couple of weeks. They found her body on May 19th. I went back to work on June 5th."

I was sketching a timeline on my notepad. "You said that you started to drink heavily. When was that?"

"It was a gradual thing. I didn't really notice it until October, I guess. That's when things started to get real bad between Linda and me."

"And the pills?"

"Around the same time."

"Where did you get them?"

"A friend at work."

"Name?"

He shook his head. "No. I won't tell you that."

I glanced over at Julian. He had his eyes closed and didn't seem annoyed by Hovarth's answer, so I skipped over it.

"What kind of pills?"

"It was a variety of things. Pain pills, anti-depressants, speed. Probably others, too. I didn't always know."

"How about your breakdown? When did that occur?"

"March. Early in March."

"Was there any event that precipitated the breakdown? Anything that changed suddenly?"

"No, nothing?"

"And the gun? Linda, when did you find the gun?"

She reached into her purse and pulled out a diary. After flipping through it for a minute she looked up at me. "March 21st. In the morning. I confronted Donald with it on the 24th, three days ago."

"Okay. Julian, do you have any questions?"

He opened his eyes and grinned. "Maybe a couple of details, nothing important. Perhaps you'd like to take Mrs. Hovarth into the kitchen for a cup of tea."

So, he had something. "Certainly. Linda, would you join me?" For a second, I thought she was going to refuse, but she stood up and picked up her pocketbook.

"Some tea would be nice," she said. "Donald, holler if you need me."

We settled down in the kitchen and discussed her work. She was a legal secretary for a firm downtown and I made some notes, names and numbers mostly, in case the investigation happened to steer in that direction. It never did, so I won't bore you with the details.

We were on our third cup of Earl Grey when Julian and Donald joined us. My husband seemed his happy self but Donald looked even more depressed then when he had first shown up.

"We're all set," Julian said. "I've told Donald, we'll have to start with tracing the gun. That's going to mean police involvement, but we'll withhold your names as long as possible. If it turns out the gun was used in the commission of a crime, Donald will probably be arrested, at least as a material witness. If it comes to that, don't panic. We'll arrange legal counsel and continue the investigation."

Linda was shaking her head and frowning. She looked like someone who'd been completely beaten by life. I felt sorry for both of them and did my best to reassure them as they left, but I don't think it did any good.

I saw them to the elevator, then closed and locked the door. Julian was on the phone when I returned to the living room.

"Yes, Inspector Rodriguez, please, this is Julian West....... He's not? All right, when he calls in, could you ask him to drop by the penthouse? I have something for him. Thank you, sergeant."

When he hung up the phone, I glared at him. "Okay, give. What did you catch that I didn't?"

"Inflection, dear, inflection. It was in his voice, when you asked him about his breakdown. He said that there was no precipitating event and he was clearly lying."

"Did you get it?"

"Oh, yes. It seems Mr. Hovarth was having an affair. Linda doesn't know so he was reluctant to mention it in front of her. It all happened two years ago, before the death of his sister. The lady involved was Cheryl Ryan, one of the reporters at Channel 8."

"But that was two years ago. How does that bring about a breakdown now?"

"For the last eight months, Ms. Ryan has been blackmailing Donald. If he didn't help her on certain extracurricular projects then she'd produce certain photos that he hadn't been aware of, and mail them to his wife."

"What kind of extracurricular projects?"

"Getting certain powerful individuals on film in compromising positions."

"And where does this lead to the breakdown?"

"A little over a month ago, he decided that he had had enough. He told her to go climb a tree. She stormed out with the intention of mailing those photos to Linda. He's been waiting for the shoe to drop ever since."

I thought it over for a minute. "Could she have planted that gun for some reason?"

"It's possible. One detail, however, must be considered."

"Which is?"

"On March 19th, Cheryl Ryan went out on a story for Channel 8. She hasn't been seen since."

Inspector Victor Rodriguez is somewhere between thirty and one million years old, I've never been able to tell. He's been an Inspector with Homicide South as long as I've been in a position to know and as far as I can tell, he may have been around at the turn of the previous century, when Teddy Roosevelt was chief of police.

When there's no case going, our relationship with him is very cordial. In fact, we've even had him up to dinner a few times. But he has a real problem with the way Julian works, and during business exchanges, things can get pretty heated. He's yet to go as far as hauling us in for withholding evidence, but I'm convinced it's only a matter of time.

This time, he didn't know we had a case, so when he showed up around dinnertime he was in a good mood. We exchanged pleasantries and as I brought him into the living room, he asked, "So, what's up?"

I pointed at the bundle on the coffee table. We had rewrapped it, but otherwise, it was just as Hovarth had left it. "Be careful undoing the bundle," I said, "you don't want to smudge any prints."

He scowled at the package and sat down on the couch. "Another one of your games, huh? Who's your client?"

"No comment." I crossed my arms and stood there, staring at him.

"Humph!" He looked at the bundle for another minute or so, and then carefully unwrapped it. When he saw the gun, his scowl got deeper and his face started to flush. "All right, where did you get it?"

"We're withholding that for now."

"Like hell you are! Where's that husband of yours? If he thinks he can pull this off, he's finally lost his mind. I want to know where this came from and I want to know right now."

"Victor, please. It might not be important at all. Just run the gun. If it turns out that it's been used for something illegal, and you can prove it, we'll cooperate. Within reason."

"Within reason, my ass! Get Julian out here."

"He's not here."

"Well where is he?" Rodriguez's face was getting redder by the minute and his voice was starting to turn hoarse.

"He knew you were going to behave like this, so he went out. He said to tell you that he'd give you a call tomorrow afternoon to see if you came up with anything."

Rodriguez didn't know what to do. He looked at me, looked around the room, looked back at the gun. Finally, without saying a word, he wrapped up the gun and left, slamming the door on the way out.

When I was sure he had left, I walked into the theater room where Julian was watching the latest James Bond movie. "Did he take it?"

"Not happily, but yeah, he took it. What now?"

"Tomorrow morning we'll take a trip down to Channel 8. I'd like to wait until we find out about the gun, but I don't think we have that luxury."

Turns out it didn't matter. At 2am, Rodriguez was back at our door, this time with a warrant. Cheryl Ryan's body had been found, shot twice with a .38 revolver. Guess which one?

"Where did you get the gun?"

We were sitting in Inspector Rodriguez's office at Homicide South. We weren't cuffed and we weren't in a cell, but we were both under arrest all the same. It was almost dawn and I was exhausted, but Julian looked wide-awake.

He folded his hands behind his head and let out a sigh. "I've told you twenty times, Victor. If you let me call my client and ask him to come in on his own, I'll tell you all about it. I promise that I won't tell him to run for it. You can even sit right here and listen to the conversation."

Rodriguez turned to me. "What about you? You got any more sense than he has?"

"Nope, not a bit."

He snarled, but I could see the gears turning in his head. Finally, he slid the phone across his desk and growled, "Call!"

Julian smiled and reached for the phone. In a moment our client was on the other end. "Donald? This is Julian West. I'm afraid that situation we discussed as a possibility has come to fruition. I'm in an office at Homicide South. Yes, homicide. Cheryl Ryan has been murdered, with that gun. No, actually, Donald, I'm quite convinced of your innocence, and I'll do my best to prove it. But the police want to see you. Now. I'm afraid it's unavoidable. Brush your teeth, have yourself a decent breakfast, and come on in. Ask for Inspector Rodriguez's office. Right, see you soon."

Julian hung up the phone and turned to Rodriguez. "He'll be here in about an hour. Now, I'll be happy to tell you everything I know, if you'll answer a few questions first."

"Dammit, West..."

"Hold on, I'm not asking a lot, just a few details. I'll get them anyway, you know that."

"What?"

"Where was the body found?"

"In the basement of Channel 8. Behind an air conditioning unit."

"Killed somewhere else?"

"Yes!" Rodriguez was spitting out his answers.

"Any idea where?"

"Somewhere in the building."

"Million-dollar question, when was she killed?"

"March 19th. The day she disappeared."

Julian grinned and leaned back in his chair. Apparently, that was the answer he wanted, but damned if I could figure out why.

Then Rodriguez started asking questions, and we answered, withholding nothing. It took better than an hour and when we were finished, Donald was waiting for Rodriguez in the outer office.

After some routine assurances that we wouldn't conceal any evidence or hamper the official investigation in any way, Victor cut us loose and we were out on the street. I thought Julian would drag us home to change and get some breakfast, but instead, he hailed a cab and gave the driver the address for Channel 8.

In the cab, he whistled to himself. Whistled. He had something all right, something that he was happy about. I tried running through some of the facts in my mind. She was killed on the 19th, the gun was found on the 21st. That didn't leave much time for the killer to plant it, unless Hovarth was the killer, and Julian had proclaimed him innocent in front of Rodriguez, so that didn't seem probable.

The wife? Maybe Linda had found out about the affair. But if that was it, why were we headed to Channel 8? I could have just asked Julian, but I've developed this theory that every time I admit that he's caught something that I missed, his head gets just a little bigger. Since I don't want to deal with the consequences of that, I suffer in silence. Sooner or later, it all comes out.

At Channel 8, Julian produced a business card and asked to see the station manager. With police still buzzing all over the place and everybody working on putting together the noon broadcast, it was almost eleven when we were ushered into Simon Richards' office.

Richards was a soft looking man, with rounded edges. He reminded me of the station manager on the TV show WKRP in Cincinnati. Except for the hair. Richards had a full head of bright red hair. Very full. It looked sort of like a dead fox lying on his head.

He was on the phone when we came in, so we sat down in front of his desk and waited. "No, I don't care what she's got on the hook," he told the phone. "No. I'm not authorizing one foot of film until she shows me an outline. I don't care how they do things at WGAL, she's at 8 now and she's going to do things our way." He slammed the phone down on his desk. "God damn prima donnas! Who the hell are you?"

Julian cleared his throat and I had to swallow a chuckle. Maybe I'd have to revise my opinion about Mr. Richards. He might look like Mr. Carlson, but he sounded like Perry White. Julian produced another card and introduced us.

"Private detectives," Richards sneered. "As if we haven't had enough of the public kind around today. West? I've heard of you, haven't I? The O'Donnell thing last year. You made a real monkey out of the cop in charge of that one, didn't you? What's he doing now, cleaning toilets? Never mind, what do you want?"

"Just a few questions, Mr. Richards," Julian said. "How well did you know Cheryl Ryan?"

"I've already gone over this with the police. I knew Cheryl on a professional basis only, and even that was a little strained. She wasn't a very likeable person and she had her own way of doing things."

"How long had she been with Channel 8?"

"Since before I took over. Four years, I think."

"When did you take over?"

"Two and a half years ago."

"Who knew her well?"

Richards tapped a pencil on his desk and sighed. "Donald Hovarth, her cameraman. Nick Draber, her soundman. Maybe Alice McGwyer, she's another reporter. Katie Bartell, she's an intern here. She works with Alice and Cheryl, depending on what's going on. I think they were friends."

"Who was running the camera for Cheryl while Mr. Hovarth was out?"

"The intern. Katie."

"On the 19th, she was on her way out on a story. Where was she going?"

"I don't know."

Julian raised an eyebrow. "She didn't tell anyone?"

"Not as far as I know."

Julian was quiet for a minute, so I stuck in my two cents. "What about the intern?"

Richards shook his head. "No. Cheryl would usually run down the details on a story by herself, and then bring out a camera. It was more cost effective and people talked to her easier if she was alone."

Julian was up and offering his head. "It's been a pleasure meeting you Mr. Richards. It's been a long day for us, already, and we really need to get some food and some rest. Could I ask you a favor?"

"What is it?"

"Could you ask a couple of your people to call on me this evening? Say eight o'clock?"

Richards was frowning. "Who?"

"Alice McGwyer and Nick Draber. Oh, and the intern, what was her name?"

"Katie Bartell."

"Right, Ms. Bartell. Well?"

"I'll ask them, but I won't insist."

"That would be wonderful. Thanks again."

I'll skip over the afternoon, as it didn't hold anything that would interest you unless you're intrigued by what Julian or I wear to bed, and if that's what you want, I think you bought the wrong magazine. I'll just say that we had a brief lunch and got about four hours of shuteye, before the alarm went off at 6 that evening.

After a quick shower, we both dressed and started prepping the living room, making sure everyone had a comfortable place to sit and stocking the portable bar. I slapped together some finger sandwiches and put them out on the coffee table while Julian put in a new blank tape and tested the hidden recording system.

Satisfied that everything was in place, we were just about to mix ourselves something to drink when the doorman buzzed to let us know that our first guest had arrived.

Fifteen minutes later they had all arrived, and I was serving the last of them, Alice McGwyer, a scotch and soda. As I mixed their drinks, I hadn't formed any conclusions, but at least I had a better picture of each of them.

The first to arrive had been Katie Bartell, the intern. A little older than I had expected, maybe 27 or 28, she had short blonde hair and an overly serious expression, although that could have been due to the circumstances. I wasn't really expecting business dress that time of night, but she wore battered old jeans and an Alanis Morrissette concert shirt, which, I decided, was a deliberate attempt to look casual. She drank beer.

Next came Nick Draber and he was more like what I expected. Mid 30's, long hair pulled back in a neat ponytail. Khaki's, loafers and a polo shirt with the Channel logo on the breast. He was polite, but outgoing and he smiled a lot. His teeth needed work. He asked for, and drank, bourbon, straight up.

Last was Alice McGwyer, and as I already pointed out, she drank scotch and soda. Unlike the others, there was nothing casual about Alice's outfit. A flaming red, silk blouse, black, hip-hugging mini skirt, black stockings and stiletto heels. Ms. McGwyer obviously had plans for the evening and our penthouse was just a pit stop.

Once they were all seated and served, Julian made his entrance. Introducing himself, he followed his normal routine, handshake for the man, a kiss of the hand for the ladies. He told me once that he did that to see how people would react to the unexpected, and even though I don't really buy that, I watched their reactions carefully. Katie took it with no fuss and a look of mild surprise, as it should be. Alice, on the other hand, giggled and almost swooned.

I decided that I didn't like her. Maybe she'd turn out to be the killer. I crossed my toes.

After the introductions, they all wanted to speak. It was the usual stuff, why were they here, what was going on, who did Julian think he was?

Eventually, he got them settled down enough to answer them. "First, let me thank you all for coming. You are all aware that I'm a private agent and you have no legal compulsion to be here, so I am grateful for your sufferance. As to who I think I am, that's obvious, I'm Julian West. To what's going on, that too is obvious. I'm investigating a murder. Why are you here? Because I think you can help me unmask the killer."

Nick Draber interrupted, "but the police already have the killer. Don Hovarth."

"No, sir. For reasons of my own, I've concluded that Mr. Hovarth is innocent. Therefore, we must look elsewhere. As three of Ms. Ryan's closest colleagues, you are undoubtedly aware of much that I am not, and I need that information. For example, Ms. Bartell, did Ms. Ryan tell you anything about the story she was working on?"

"Nothing," she replied. "I didn't even know she was working on something. I had been doing some copy editing for Alice."

"On what project was that? Ms. McGwyer?"

"A story on the school system for the Children Matter series. I had it scripted out at six minutes but Richards wanted it cut to four and a half."

"Is it usual to have an intern do your copy editing?"

Alice smiled at him. Coy. I hate coy. "Not often, but Katie's been with us over a year and she's handled that sort of thing before. It all depends on how busy I am."

"Mr. Draber? Would you know about a piece in advance? I'm not familiar with your procedures."

"In advance? No. Most of my work is done in the studio, after the fact. Every once in a while, a piece will need some on site sound work, but that's usually same day prep. Never advance notice."

"Did you ever see Ms. Ryan outside of the studio?"

Nick grinned. "Frequently. We used to date."

"Indeed. When was that?"

"Well, it started about a year and a half ago, maybe a little more. Right after she ditched Donald Hovarth. It never really ended, just sort of fizzled out. We'd still go out occasionally, maybe once a month."

"So you knew about Ms. Ryan's affair with Donald Hovarth?"

"Sure, everybody did."

Julian looked back and forth, from Nick to Alice to Katie and back again. "Is that accurate? Did you all know?"

"Yeah," Alice said, "I knew. They didn't really try to hide it."

"Well, I didn't know," Katie interrupted. "I didn't pay any attention to that sort of thing. It was none of my business."

Julian smiled at her. "Of course not. As an intern, you probably don't have the time to involve yourself in such matters."

"I wouldn't anyway. It's distasteful."

"Adultery usually is. Did you ever see Ms. Ryan, outside of the studio?"

"No."

Julian turned to Alice. "How about you? Did you associate with Ms. Ryan outside of work?"

"Sometimes. We'd go clubbing on Friday nights, when neither of us had something else on."

Julian stopped for a moment and looked them over. He was considering something, but I couldn't tell what. Chances are, I'll never be able to tell what he's thinking in those kinds of situations, but I keep trying. Anyway, after a minute, he said, "A hypothetical question for all of you. Let's assume that Cheryl Ryan was involved in something illegal and had been for some time. Who would she tell? Who would she confide in?"

They stared at us for a moment, then at each other, each turning it over in their head for their own reasons.

"I don't believe it," Katie said. "She would never..."

"I can't believe you'd even suggest that," Alice said. "You ought to be charged with libel."

"John Austin," Nick muttered.

Julian's eyes focused on him like a laser. "Who?"

"John Austin. He's an anchor at the station. He had gone to broadcast school with Cheryl, they'd been friends for years. She told him everything. The day after our first date he gave me the best friend don't you ever hurt her speech. Before I'd even had my first cup of coffee. I felt like poking him in the eye. Yeah, if she told anybody, it'd be him."

"Thank you. Ms. McGwyer, do you concur?"

"You should be ashamed of yourself. Even suggesting it. I'm going to consult the station lawyer tomorrow. I think this is actionable, and if it is, you'll be sorry." She stood up and headed for the front door, storming across and out.

"Nice exit," I mumbled and Nick let out a laugh.

"Well I don't think it's funny," Katie said. "Sure, she over reacted, but the idea that Cheryl was behind anything criminal, well, that's just ridiculous."

"Ridiculous or not," Julian answered, "It happens to be true. Cheryl Ryan was involved in a criminal scheme and it got her killed. I'll speak to Mr. Austin tomorrow, perhaps he can shed some light on her endeavors. Mr. Draber, Ms. Bartell, I thank you for your assistance. I may need to speak with you again, but not until I've answered a few questions. Good night."

Julian quickly left the room and I saw Nick and Katie to the door. Once they were on their way down, I followed my husband into the kitchen, where he was on the phone.

"Yes, Linda," he said, "I understood how you must feel. It's a deplorable way to find out about your husband's behavior. But whatever else he may have done; you must believe me; your husband is no killer. No. He's not responsible for her death. Now listen, I need some information from you. How old was Donald's sister when she died? Really? Was she a college graduate? Indeed. And what did she do for a living? Ahh. Thank you. I think I'll have some good news for you soon. Yes, you too. Good night."

He hung up the phone and looked at me, unable to suppress a grin. "Cindy Hovarth was a photographer."

I suppose that the significance of the statement seems obvious to you, but at the time, it went right over my head. I tried to question Julian about it, but he got into one of his haughty moods and just told me to think about it.

Which I did.

All night.

Lying in bed, staring at the ceiling, I turned the pieces over and over in my head, but I couldn't make them fit. How did Hovarth's sister get pulled into this mess? I thought it was about the TV station. Deciding that Julian was actually full of shit, I pulled the cover up over my head and drifted off.

I'm not sure how much sleep I actually got, but when I woke up, I could hear Julian puttering around in the kitchen. I climbed up and out of bed and forced myself into the shower, where I finally managed to get my eyes all the way open. When I eventually made it into the kitchen, awake and dressed, Julian was just finishing breakfast. He sat an omelet in front of me, gave me a quick kiss and said, "Good morning. Sleep well?"

"No and no. Why do you have to be a morning person? It's irritating."

"I'm not a morning person, I'm just me. And it's not that early dear, it's almost 10."

"Whatever. What's on today's agenda?"

"A trip to Channel 8 to see John Austin. If he can answer one or two little questions, we might be able to wrap this up today."

We get The Times and The Post delivered daily. Julian looks at them occasionally, but I try to go through them every morning. Before I had met Julian, I was a writer for The Post and I think that'll always be in my blood.

Which is just to explain why I was flipping through the paper while I listened to Julian and ate my breakfast. I had skimmed the front page once, and it hadn't registered, at least not on the surface. Then for some reason, it sunk in. I stopped chewing and turned back to the front. There it was, bottom half of the page, in big block letters.

TV ANCHOR FOUND DEAD IN HOME.

The article itself had few details, but then the body had just been discovered shortly before the paper went to press. John Austin, six o'clock anchor for Channel 8, was found dead in his home on Long Island. Shot once in the head. A sidebar pointed out that another reporter for Channel 8 had been found murdered earlier this week, but no connection was drawn between the two cases.

I must have sat there in mid-chew for a while, because Julian noticed. Without a word, he walked behind me and looked down, over my shoulder, at the article.

"She did it," he muttered. "Draber pointed him out last night and she left here and killed him. She's folding up, trying to erase all the evidence. Getting ready to cut and run."

I looked at the pieces again, trying to make them fit. I could narrow it down to two of them now, that was obvious, but which one and why? It still looked like a muddled mess and to be honest, I had no idea what was going on and said so.

"Call Mrs. Hovarth," he said. "Get her here. Now. I have some questions that can't wait."

"Tell me about Cindy. How was her relationship with Donald before her death? Were they close?"

Linda was seated on the couch once again, across from Julian. I had a chair off to the side, where I could see them both. She thought about Julian's question before answering.

"I'm honestly not sure," she said. "At one time, before she graduated, I would have said yes without hesitation. But later?" She shook her head. "I just don't know. She was a wonderful photographer and Donald had always encouraged her to go into photojournalism. But that last year in school, she got involved with some radical group. Anti-government, anti-corporation and anti-men. It was all she talked about. Everything was a conspiracy to her."

"Was she still affiliated with this group when she died?"

"No. She got disenchanted with them, shortly before graduation. Her and a friend. They moved here to New York together. I'm trying to remember her name, but I'm not sure Cindy ever told me."

"When was this, Mrs. Hovarth?"

"When they moved here? Let me see, it was about two months before Cindy's accident. Maybe three."

"This friend, did you ever meet her?" Julian was sitting forward in his chair, eagerly awaiting each answer.

"No, I never actually met her..."

Julian sighed and leaned back.

"Of course, I do have that picture."

"Picture?"

"Of Cindy and her together. Let me see, I think it's still in my purse." She rummaged through her handbag until she came out with a wallet, one of those with the little, folding plastic, picture holders. Unfolding it, she produced a photograph and handed it to Julian. "The one on the left is Cindy."

He took one look at the picture and broke out in a wide grin. Handing it to me, he asked, "well?"

A quick glance was enough. "I'll be damned. Okay, what now?"

"We have a party. Call Victor."

The key turned out to be the timeline. Going back over it, I'm surprised I didn't catch on earlier, but sometimes, when you're looking for one kind of fact, the other kind can slide right by you. But I'm getting ahead of myself.

We had a full house. Julian had brought out some extra chairs from the den and we needed them. Per Julian's request, Victor had brought our client with him, along with a couple of uniform officers to keep things under control.

Also in the living room were Linda Hovarth, Nick Draber, Alice McGwyer, Katie Bartell and Simon Richards, the station manager. It had taken me nearly a half hour to get everyone seated and refreshments passed out. They were starting to get impatient when Julian finally made his entrance.

"Thank you all for coming. I realize this is a tough time for most of you and I appreciate your forbearance. One little detail, although Inspector Rodriguez and two of his colleagues are present, they are here as observers, just like you. This is not an officially sanctioned inquiry. Is that clear enough, Victor?"

"For now," Rodriguez growled.

"Very well. I guess we should go back to the beginning, if this is to make any sense. Two years ago, Mr. Donald Hovarth had an affair with Cheryl Ryan. He managed to keep it hidden from his wife, but at the station, it was pretty much common knowledge, as Nick and Alice both pointed out yesterday evening.

"By the way, Ms. Bartell?" He turned to look at the intern. "When the subject came up last evening, you said that you weren't aware of the affair, didn't you?"

"Yes."

"But in fact, you weren't even employed at the station yet, were you? You were still in school?"

"Maybe that's why I don't remember it. I'm not very good with dates."

"That must be it. Anyway, back to the story. Although he had managed to keep the affair a secret from his wife, his sister Cindy, who was away at college, knew all about it. Donald and Cindy had been close for many years. They trusted each other completely. So perhaps he confided his guilty secret to her. Maybe he had to. Keeping illicit rendezvous, a secret is difficult work and it would be much easier with a confederate to help cover for you. Was that why you told her, Donald?"

Our client nodded. "I'd tell Linda that I was visiting Cindy. If she called, Cindy would make up some excuse for me not being able to come to the phone."

"Trusting your sister was your biggest mistake, Donald, because Cindy had made a friend at school. For ease, let's call her Jane Doe. Jane was a radical, a member of at least one fringe group on campus. She was also a couple of years older than most college seniors. Maybe she liked life on campus, or maybe the activities took up so much of her time that she had to stretch her credits out over a longer period. It doesn't really matter.

"What does matter, is that Cindy told her about Donald's affair. Cindy knew where the lovers met, perhaps at a motel outside of the city, and she told Jane that, also. Somehow, Jane talked Cindy into accompanying her to that motel, and into bringing her camera. They photographed Donald and Cheryl in the act.

"Now we move forward several months. Cindy and Jane have moved to New York and Jane has managed to get a job at Channel 8, to be close to her subjects. She's ready to put her plan into motion, but Cindy objects. Maybe she had a change of heart, or maybe she had never known just what Jane had intended to do with those photographs. But she threatened to disrupt Jane's plan, maybe even to turn her in.

"So Jane killed her. She hit her on the back of the head and dropped her in a tub full of water. The death was recorded as an accidental drowning.

"And Jane was free to continue with her plan. First, she approached Cheryl Ryan. She told her that she was going to use her position to dig up blackmail material on wealthy citizens. That if Cheryl would help, she would cut her in for a piece of the pie. If not, well she had these photographs.

"They decide that they need a good cameraman, so Cheryl approaches Donald, using the photographs as leverage. She doesn't tell him about Jane Doe. He agrees, reluctantly, to protect himself. But after several months of guilt and buoyed by alcohol and pills, he tells Cheryl to shove it. He won't do it anymore and if she continues, he'll go to the police.

"Cheryl panics and goes to Jane Doe. Actually, I've had enough of this Jane Doe stuff. We all know who I'm talking about. Cheryl panicked and went to Ms. Katie Bartell."

The intern was steadily shaking her head. "No. You can't prove that. You can't prove any of it."

Julian reached into his shirt pocket and pulled out the photograph, handing it to Inspector Rodriguez. "This is a picture of Cindy Hovarth and Katie Bartell, at school together. If you dig a bit, I'm sure you'll find more physical evidence to support my story. Should I continue?"

Victor nodded, "Yes."

"With Cheryl in a panic and Donald ready to go to the police, Katie realized that the operation was falling down around her. But Donald only knew about Cheryl, not her. So, by eliminating Cheryl and framing Donald for it, her problem would be solved. A question, just for neatness' sake, Donald, did your sister have a key to your home?"

"Yes"

"I'm betting it wasn't found in her possessions. That's how Katie got the gun into your house. Her killing spree probably would have ended there if Nick hadn't mentioned John Austin last night. Knowing that he might know all about her, Katie couldn't let him live.

I should have realized that last night and if I had, Mr. Austin would still be here now."

Rodriguez stood up and looked at Katie. "Ms. Bartell, do you have anything to say for yourself?"

"It's all a pack of lies."

"Even the photograph." Rodriguez shook his head. "No, I don't think so. You have the right to remain silent…"

You might be wondering about our fee on this one, since Donald and Linda obviously weren't loaded. It seems that Ms. Bartell had rented a post office box where all the blackmail payments were being sent.

Julian asked for and received permission to draft a letter to send to everyone who was sending money to that P.O. Box.

The letter detailed the case and told the blackmail victims that the blackmailer was safely behind bars, her tapes had been destroyed and there would be no more demands for payment.

The letter closed with the following statement:

If you would like to show your gratitude for the service that has been rendered to you, you can send checks to the following address, payable to Julian West.

So far, our net on the case has topped one hundred thousand, and a new check just arrived yesterday. Go figure.

Decisions

The old man sat in the dimly lit bar, thinking about his past. He had a lit cigarette in front of him, but it sat untouched in the ashtray and he watched the curls of smoke drift away from it. The bartender eyed him, but did not ask if he wanted a drink. The old man had been coming into the bar every day for a month now, and it was always the same. He'd light a cigarette, but not smoke it. He'd stare at the bottles behind the wall and his eyes would drift into the past. He never ordered a drink.

Until today. "Scotch, please. Neat."

The bartender nodded and poured his drink.

"What's your name, son?" The old man asked.

"Eddie." He said it hesitantly, unsure how much he wanted to reveal to the old man.

"It's all about choices, wouldn't you say, Eddie?"

"I'm not sure I follow you."

The old man chuckled. It was a dry, rasping, hideous noise. "Every step of the way, Eddie. Every choice we make, it defines who we are. Like that girl in Austin, back in '62. That could have worked ·out differently. It was my choice, you know. I chose the bottle. Son, I always choose the bottle.

"I had a son, once, long time ago. Wasn't worth much, but that was probably my fault. Killed himself over a woman. Probably for the best. Like I said, he wasn't worth much. Saved me the trouble."

"The Trouble?" Eddie was getting more and more uneasy.

"Then there was that hooker in Reno. Such a shame, really. Pretty girl."

"I'm not sure I understand this, sir."

"They're dead, Eddie. They're all dead. Decisions, Decisions."

"How do you make such an awful decision," Eddie gasped.

"Well, son," the old man smiled, "the scotch usually helps."

And Eddie noticed the long-handled knife that now lay atop the bar…

I Am Prepared To Bear Your Company And Do It With A Thankful Heart

It was Christmas Eve in Frankfort, Michigan and The Mariner was empty but for me and an off-duty cop named Dan Avery. Dan represented one third of the city's police department and I, Nick Kellerman, its sole private detective. We were drinking Jim Beam and discussing the presents we had purchased for our respective girlfriends.

My girl, Sasha, was only 20, and since I'm pushing 40, Dan's end of the conversation included a lot of jokes about cradles and playpens. I took it in good humor, only occasionally threatening to spank him with my cane. In truth, the situation made me feel awkward, but Sasha felt it was perfectly acceptable, so what did I know?

We were starting to come to the conclusion that neither one of us was very good at gift buying when Susie Vandrick, who worked in the flower shop below my office, burst in and started babbling about a body down on the beach. Dan calmed her down and the bartender brought her a cup of hot coffee. It took a while, but we got what details we could from her. She said the body was on the beach, just off the turnaround at the end of the road. Dan and I threw on our coats and went for a walk.

The Mariner sat almost at the end of the main road and the only thing between it and the beach at Lake Michigan was a few condos and the turnaround. It had been snowing off and on for two weeks by then and the beach was covered in several inches of bright clean snow. A field of white broken only by the body lying in the middle of it. A single set of footprints, presumably his own, led from the turnaround to the body.

It was a male, probably in his mid-thirties, with broad shoulders and sandy hair.

"Any idea who it is?" Dan asked.

"No," I lied.

The next hour was a flurry of activity. I walked out to the body and verified that he was really dead while Dan went back to his car and called it in. There was no blood, no visible injuries. I checked his fingernails and lips, smelled his breath. No obvious signs of foul play, could have been a heart attack or stroke. The ambulance showed up first, then the rest of Frankfort 's police department and at least they were actually sober and on duty unlike Dan.

We backed off and let them take over. Dan went back to The Mariner to finish his drink. I went home to think things over.

Sasha was there when I got home, curled up on the couch watching an old movie on TV. I had given her a key a few months ago and she was there more often than not now, which always made me smile. Even her parents approved, which is an odd thing to be thinking about at my age, but, truthfully, it was starting to make me feel younger.

After a quick kiss and a few minutes of small talk I told her about the incident at the beach. She raised an eyebrow when I told her that I had lied to Dan and she outright scowled when I pulled the dead man's wallet from my pocket.

"You stole his wallet?"

"Well, yeah."

"Why?"

"So Dan wouldn't find it. I needed to slow down the identification process."

She stared at me like she always does when she wants me to know that I'm not making any sense. She thinks it looks irritating; I think it looks adorable. Don't tell her.

"So," she said, "You don't want the body identified?"

"Not yet."

"Why? No, don't tell me, you have to be the one to solve the case, even if there isn't a case. You know you're a very weird man, don't you?"

I grinned at her. "I've always suspected."

She turned off the TV and sat down at the kitchen table with me while I examined his wallet. "Who is he?" she asked.

"When he came to see me at the office, he claimed his name was John Leech, but his license says James Reed. Traverse City address." I flipped through the billfold. "Credit cards, lot of cash, just over two grand."

"Why the fake name?"

"Lots of people use fake names with P.I.'s. Doesn't necessarily mean anything."

She thought about it for a minute, and then stood up. "I'm going to fix us a couple of drinks."

"You're too young to drink."

"Bite me, old man." She poured us each a shot of Canadian Whiskey over ice and sat back down. "What did he want, anyway?"

"Well, he wanted me to get the ghosts to leave him alone."

"Ghosts?"

"Yeah, the ghosts of Christmas, past, present and future."

"You're kidding?"

"Nope. That's what he wanted." The whiskey went down smooth. Sasha noticed my glass was empty and refilled it. She had barely touched hers. I could never figure out how she could do that.

"So, what did you tell him?"

"I gave him the number of a good shrink up in Interlochen."

"And now you're feeling guilty?"

"I'm always feeling guilty about something, that's beside the point. Think about the story. A Christmas Carol is all about guilt and last-minute redemption, trying to salvage your life before it's too late."

"So, you think the ghost delusion came from feelings of guilt?"

"And possibly a desire to atone for that guilt. Maybe a desire that was being blocked somehow."

She went into the living room and retrieved her laptop. She had set me up with a wireless internet service over the fall, but she was the only one who ever really used it. I still had trouble doing anything more than paying my bills or reading my email. In a few minutes she had it fired up and was surfing through various information sites.

"John Leech was an artist," she muttered. "He did the original drawings for A Christmas Carol."

I wandered over to my bookshelves and pulled my copy down. She was right, of course. I flipped through the illustrations. They reminded me a bit of Sidney Paget's Sherlock Holmes drawings.

I put the book away and returned to the table.

"Got him," she announced. "James Reed, he's an accountant for a medical research firm in Traverse. He's been indicted for embezzlement, he's due to appear in court on the 26th. Or he was, anyway. Could have been looking at twenty years."

"And he probably knew he was going to be convicted, so he came down here to make amends."

"To whom?"

"That's what we need to find out." I pulled a key from my pocket.

"What's that?" Sasha asked.

"A car key. For a BMW."

"You lifted that off his body, too?"

I grinned. "Yep."

"You're going to get in a lot of trouble one of these days. Let me get my coat"

There were more BMW's in downtown Frankfort than I expected. It took almost two hours to find the right one, a late model silver Z4, parked down main street near the library. Sasha sat inside and flipped through the glove compartment while I checked the trunk.

I found a black leather attaché case, locked of course. I closed the trunk and climbed into the driver's seat, case in hand. "Find any little keys?" I asked.

"No, just an empty snickers wrapper and a sheet of note paper with a name and an address. Debbie Kingsley, on Leelanau."

"Hmm." I pulled out my pocketknife and went to work on the lock. Sasha watched me, amused. In a few minutes I had managed to cut two fingers and twist the knife up like a pretzel. For some reason, Sasha thought this was hysterical.

I gave up and we walked back to my house, case and notepaper with us. Armed with a power drill, I had the case open in just a few minutes. I'm not sure what I was expecting to find inside, but it wasn't money.

"How much do you think it is?" Sasha asked.

I shook my head. "Twenty grand, fifty grand. Hard to tell without counting."

"Drug deal?"

"With jail time fast coming up? Not likely."

"A payoff then. To make amends for past wrongs?"

I nodded. "Probably. We should go talk to Ms. Kingsley."

"We?"

"Well, you're always curious about what I do. This one seems to be pretty harmless."

"Except for the dead body on the beach."

"Well, yes, except for that."

"Let me change first." I watched her walk up the stairs and waited. She came back a few minutes later, sweatshirt and jeans replaced with a sweater and dark slacks. It seemed natural to me that she kept her clothes in my home, that she could change here. It was a feeling I hadn't experienced since my divorce.

"Are you happy, Sasha? Here, with me?"

"Of course, I wouldn't be here otherwise." She put her arms around my waist and gave me a kiss.

"You don't feel like you're missing something, that you went right from teenager to adult?"

"Oh yeah, I'm missing all those years of angst and uncertainty. No thanks, I like my life just fine."

I smiled. "Well, then, let's go to work."

The Kingsley house was a dilapidated old thing, with overgrown grass and peeling yellow paint. Sasha looked about nervously as we approached the door and I put an arm around her shoulder reassuringly. The lady who answered the door was no one to be frightened of. Blonde, exhausted and old before her years. I expected a cigarette to be dangling between her lips, but there was no sign of one.

"What do you want?" she asked.

"Mrs. Kingsley?"

"Ms. Kingsley. But, yeah, that's me."

"I'd like to ask you a few questions about James Reed?"

Her face darkened with anger. "Tell that bastard to stay away from me and Jessie. We don't want nothing to do with him, ever again."

"We can't do that, ma'am," Sasha said.

"Why not?"

"Because he's dead."

That took the wind right out of her sails. She seemed to deflate as she stepped back and motioned us in. I had the money from the briefcase in an old gym bag and I kept it in my grip. She cleared a path to the living room for us. People always did that for me now, I think it's the cane.

A little girl was playing in the corner of the room, I assumed that she was Jessie.

"What happened to him?" She asked. "He was just here this morning."

"They're not sure yet. They found his body on the beach this afternoon." I thought about which way to go with the next question. "Ms. Kingsley, what did James want this morning?"

She shook her head. "I don't know, I wouldn't let him in."

"Is Jessie his daughter?" Sasha asked.

"Yes. But he hadn't seen her in years. He ran off with some tramp when she was just a little baby."

I stood up and started pacing the room. "He was going to jail, Ms. Kingsley. Can I call you Debbie? My name is Nick, by the way. This is Sasha." We said a quick round of hellos and I went back to my point. "I think he was planning to be away for a long time. He came here, to give you something for Jessie. Before I give it to you, you should know, I don't think it's in anyway traceable. The police don't know that he came here to see you, and I have no intention of telling them. He was feeling guilt, Debbie, about the way he treated you and the way he abandoned his daughter."

I handed her the gym bag. She opened it up and her eyes got wide.

"I don't know how much is there," I said. "It should be enough to help you start a new life. Take care of your daughter."

"Thank you." She was crying and the words came out garbled.

I led Sasha to the door. Time to leave her alone to deal with her own guilt. Sasha stopped at the threshold and turned back. "Debbie, did James have any allergies?"

The woman nodded. "Peanuts. They made his throat close up and he'd have to go to the hospital."

Sasha shook her head and we left.

We were sitting on my couch, fireplace going, lights down low. Her feet were tucked up under her and she leaned against me, watching the fire.

"So, the candy bar wrapper?" Sasha asked. "It was peanuts, right?"

"Right."

"Did she kill him?"

"No, it was suicide. Good catch."

"Where do the ghosts fit in? She asked.

"Well, he's obviously a fan of Dickens or that artist's name would never have come up. Maybe it was just a clever metaphor for his desire to put things right."

"Maybe he was having a nervous breakdown and the delusions were leading him along."

"We'll never know for sure."

I ran my fingers lightly through her hair. It was midnight now, Christmas morning. "I bought you a singing mouse," I said.

She looked up at me. "What?"

"A singing mouse. For Christmas."

She thought about it for a minute. "What does it sing?"

"Jingle Bell Rock."

She burst out laughing. "You're a weird guy, Nick."

I stood up and walked over to the fireplace. "Listen, Sash, we've talked a lot about your future, college, your career. There's one part of the future that we never really talk about."

"Nick…"

Sleight of Mind

"Wait. I know you've got your whole life ahead of you and I know I'm just a busted up old man..."

"You're not old."

"I'm getting there pretty damn fast. Not the point, though. What I mean to say, well, to ask...." I pulled a small black box out of my pocket and opened it up. I felt my throat catch as I got down on one knee in front of her and presented her with the open box. Inside was a diamond on a thin band of white gold.

"Sasha, will you marry me?"

She was crying, but she was also smiling when she said, "Yes."

The Ceremony of Innocence

For the late Robert B. Parker, the best there ever was.

I had come to Boston looking for a runaway and I had found her. Unfortunately, she had no interest in returning to Michigan and after listening to her story, I had no interest in telling her parents her whereabouts.

Which meant that this little trip would not only be missing a payday, but that all expenses would be coming out of my own pocket. A reality which led me to one inescapable conclusion; it was time for a beer.

I settled on a nice Irish looking pub that was only a block from my hotel. It was decorated in dark wood and lacked the endless television screens that littered most of the bars back in Benzie County.

Being mid-afternoon, the place was mostly barren. There were a few businessmen littered about, a couple of college kids skipping classes and a big guy who looked mostly like a thug sitting at the bar.

I grabbed a stool next to him, feeling more at home with thugs than business men or college kids. The bartender came over and asked to take my order. He was an older man, in formal wear, like a proper bartender. I felt like I was in an old movie, but I wasn't sure of my lines.

"What have you got on draft?" I asked.

"Wicked, Intensity, Shock Ale, Darkest Night, Phantom and Shatter."

I stared at him in shock and the big man next to me laughed. "It's a sad state of affairs when you can't tell the difference between the name of a beer and the title of the latest Dean Koontz book," he said. "Darren, give the man a bottle of Sam Adams."

I looked over at the man and said, "Thank you."

"No problem. Tastes better from the bottle, anyway."

I offered him my hand. "Nick Kellerman. I'm a private eye from Michigan."

"No shit." He reached into his pocket and pulled out a business card. "What are the odds?"

It seemed my companion was also a private detective. "Nice card."

"Thanks."

"The silhouette of the guy with the gun is a nice touch. Very James Bond."

"I thought about adding master sleuth under my name, but it seemed a bit much."

"Probably would have depended on the font. You can get away with a lot if you've got a good font."

"This is true." He took a sip of his beer and ordered another one. "What brings you to Boston?"

"Dead end case. I'm heading back tomorrow."

I realized my beer was gone and signaled the bartender for another.

"You like Sam Adams?" my new friend asked.

"Yeah. It's a solid beer, lots of flavor."

He grinned and ordered another. "I've been drinking Sam off and on for too many years to count. I'll get on various kicks, you know? Spend a month drinking Rolling Rock or Amstel. But I always come back to Samuel Adams. Tastes like home."

"I know what you mean. I drink a lot of Labatt's back in Michigan. Crisp, clean. It's a good, everyday beer. It's no Sam Adams, though."

We sat there and drank for some time, exchanging stories about cases, discovering that we had some friends in common in New York and Philadelphia. He told me about his longtime girlfriend, Susan. I told him about Sasha.

In the end, we exchanged information and declarations. If you ever need help with a case in, etc., etc. I'm not sure that I'll ever need a hand in Boston. After all, I rarely leave Michigan these days. But if I do, I know who to call.

And I doubt if he'll ever really need a hand in Northern Michigan, but if he does, I'll be glad to help out. Because we shared a night locked in an ancient ceremony, trading stories and beer and becoming, if not comrades-in-arms, then comrades in fine Boston lager.

The Hour is Getting Late

I always knew I'd be around for the end of the world.

Don't ask me how. It's not like I'm a religious man, or a superstitious one. I didn't sit around thinking about The Rapture or the prophecies of Nostradamus. I didn't spend much time thinking about it at all. I just knew that I would be there for it, that it would happen in my lifetime.

I just didn't realize that I would be locked in a padded room when it happened.

Of course, some people would tell you that's the reason I was in the padded room to begin with, but they'd be wrong. The real reason, well, I don't want to talk about the real reason I was there. It doesn't matter anymore, does it? Does anything from before matter?

Do you remember that old poem about the world ending, not with a bang, but a whimper? Locked in that room, drugged out of my mind, I didn't even hear the whimper. Just a sort of piercing silence.

No one came that day. Not the nurse that usually brought my pills or the orderly that brought my food. I noticed. I wasn't so far gone that I didn't notice, but I didn't care. I had been kept drugged for over a year, docile, pliant. That doesn't wear off in a day.

Or two. Or three.

On the fourth day, when the haze was getting thinner and the hunger was almost unbearable, I heard noise outside my room. Doors opening and closing, things being tossed about, somebody singing. Actually singing.

I sat on the edge of my bed and waited. I knew that she'd (the singing voice was definitely feminine) eventually open my door. I wondered what I'd say to her. Wondered, not planned, because I didn't think my conscious mind, still working its way through the Thorazine fog, had any hope of controlling my lips. I wasn't even sure I'd be able to talk. It had been so long.

I told her, much later, that I had spent the time wondering what she looked like. If she'd be pretty. The truth is, it never occurred to me. She didn't have that much reality in my mind. She was just a melodic voice that could open doors. I wanted her to open mine. That's all that mattered.

When she finally did open it, and I managed to stutter a simple hello, she screamed. It was loud and shrill and it went on for a long time. Minutes, hours, days, who can say anymore. Later, she told me she screamed because she thought she was alone in the world. That it was just her and the things that roamed outside. She had been searching the ward for things to make life more comfortable. I think she meant drugs, but I didn't ask. There are a lot of things I never got around to asking her. I wish I had. I wish a lot of things these days, but my head was still so foggy back then.

I never thought to ask her name.

That's the one I regret the most. She will always just be "her" to me.

I thought for some time that she would be back. She had only intended to be gone for an hour or so. I may not be able to tell you much about the passage of time, but I know that hour is long past. My beard is much thicker now. My hair much longer.

I still think about her at night, when the howling outside is at its worst and I'm wandering the halls. I can still her faintly muffled voice, singing somewhere off in my head. The words just a bit too soft to decipher.

Sometimes the melody makes me smile.

An Unexpected Box

I woke in absolute darkness.

I felt hot and sticky and unsure of just where I was, but it was the darkness that worried me the most. I don't sleep in dark rooms. It's not a fear of the dark, at least it's not just a fear of the dark. I can't navigate in the dark, you see. I'm always bumping into things, stubbing my toe on some piece of random furniture.

And I'm never sure that I'm alone.

It's not normally an issue. I don't need a night light or anything. With the light from the digital clock, the standby light on the television, the glow from the power strip, and from the DVD player, there's enough ambient light that I can see what I need to see. But there were none of those things.

The bed felt comfortable and familiar. The pillows felt like mine, and so did the blanket. Perhaps there had been a power outage. I fumbled around the headboard (also familiar), feeling for my cell phone. I could use the light from that to get my bearings. But I couldn't find it. It wasn't where I always left it, in the little inset shelf on the left side of the bed. Why wasn't it there?

I sat up, carefully, letting my legs drop from the left side of the bed. I always sleep on the left side. I live alone now, it's been five years since my wife left, but I still sleep on my side of the bed, just the same. I tried spreading out once, not long after her departure, but I couldn't get comfortable that way. So I sleep on the left, and it was on the left side that my feet dropped to the floor, which felt colder than usual.

It was November, so it was cold outside. Not wintery yet, but cold enough that the heat had been kicking on. Perhaps the power was out. There was no sound of rain, but maybe the storm had passed. I hadn't been woken by thunder though, and that usually shocks me awake.

I stood, feeling around carefully until I found my way to the wall where I knew the light switch was located. I flipped it and the room was flooded in sudden light so bright I had to shield my eyes for a moment. As my eyes became accustomed to the luminescence, I looked around. Each of my electronic items were still there, but none of them were lit up, I walked over to the television and pushed the power button.

Nothing happened.

I looked behind the TV and followed the cord back to the power strip. Still plugged in, but the strip wasn't lit up. I followed that cord back to the wall and found it was also still plugged in, just as it should have been. Perhaps a fuse had blown. Were the lights on a different fuse from the wall outlets?

I walked out of my bedroom and down the hall, flipping on light switches as I went. They all seemed to work perfectly. It was my intention to walk past my kitchen and take the stairs down to the basement to check the fuse box, but something in my peripheral vision caught my eye and I stopped cold. I looked past the kitchen into the dining room. There, sitting in the center of the table, was an unexpected black box.

I felt a sudden dread come over me, but I couldn't understand why. It would be logical, upon finding something heretofore unknown in one's home, to think that an intruder might be present, but that wasn't what I feared. In fact, it never even entered my mind. It was the box itself that inspired the dread and why would a box do that?

I walked closer to it, exercising great caution, and taking care not to touch the offending object. It wasn't overly large, maybe a foot on each side. There appeared to be no seams or openings and it wasn't made of cardboard. It had a sheen like plastic, but I wasn't willing to touch it to be sure. I tried to think of what it could be, but only two things came to my mind when I thought of mysterious black boxes, the flight recorder in a plane and the strange obelisk at the beginning of Stanley Kubrick's film, 2001: A Space Odyssey. Both options felt ludicrous and uncomfortable to me.

I backed away from the table and went back to my bedroom, in search of my cell phone. I found it on the headboard, right where it should be. I wondered why I couldn't find it earlier, but pushed the thought from my mind and pushed the button that was supposed to bring my phone to life.

Nothing happened. The screen remained black.

Still in my pajamas, I hurried through the house and out the front door into a bright new day. The sun was blazing in the sky, not a cloud in sight, and that didn't make any sense. It was still dark just a few minutes ago, or I would have been able to see just fine in my bedroom. How could so much time have passed? How long had I stood there, staring at that mysterious box?

I knew I needed help and if my phone wouldn't work, I would go to a neighbor's house and ask to use theirs. I didn't really know any of my neighbors, even though I had lived in the same house for over a decade no, surely one would be kind enough to let me use their phone in an emergency?

If I could explain myself. Perhaps they wouldn't understand. Would an unexpected box constitute an emergency to them? I was trying to work out how I would explain the problem as I crossed the street in front of my house, when I glanced down at the cell phone in my hand and saw light. It was on.

I looked at the screen. Everything appeared normal. I had three bars. As I stood looking at the screen, I suddenly felt cold and wet. I was standing in a puddle in the center of the road. It wasn't a busy road and I probably could have stood there a while longer without encountering any traffic, but it felt wiser to return to the curb.

I turned and stepped back the way I had come. Just before I reached the edge of the road, the phone went out. I turned again and crossed back over the road. By the time I reached that curb, my phone was back on.

"Proximity," I muttered. "If I'm close enough to the box, the phone doesn't work."

I brought up my contacts, and clicked on Cindy's name. Cindy was clever, she'd know what to do.

She answered on the third ring. "Peter? Are you okay? Where are you?"

I worked with Cindy, at the township offices, and I was never late and almost never absent, except for a couple of days around the time of my divorce. Her alarm told me that I should have been at work by now, but with the strangeness of the morning it hadn't occurred to me.

"My alarm clock isn't working," I said.

"I've tried calling you four times, it kept going straight to voicemail."

"Neither is my phone. At least it wasn't working in the house."

"What?" Cindy sounded confused. "Are you okay? Are you coming in?"

"Can you come round to my house, Cindy? I think I need some help."

"What's wrong?"

"There's a box on my kitchen table."

"What kind of box?"

"A black one."

The tone of my voice must have unsettled her because there was a moment's silence and then Cindy said that she'd be right over. I watched the screen as I walked back to my house. It went dark as I stepped out of the road, but I kept watching it all the way back inside. As I expected, it stayed dark. I pushed a few buttons, but nothing happened.

I walked into my living room and dropped it onto the coffee table. Or rather, where the coffee table should have been. I watched as the phone fell to the carpeted floor, and looked at the coffee table, which was now about two feet to the left of where it had been. For some reason, that struck me as funny, but my laugh came out sounding hollow and fake. I sat on the couch and waited for Cindy to arrive.

While I waited, I looked around the room and made a mental list of the various discrepancies between what the room was like when I went to bed last night and what it was like now. Some of them, like the coffee table, were minor and easy to explain. Others seemed impossible.

There was a knock on the front door and I knew it was Cindy. It was far too early for it to be her, she would have to have found someone to cover the phones, made it to the garage and retrieved her car, and driven all the way across town, which is normally a forty minute commute, all in the space of what could only have been ten minutes since I had spoken with her.

None of that mattered though. When I opened that door I knew exactly what I'd see. Short and curly black hair and John Lennon glasses atop a force of nature. She was only a little younger than my thirty-nine years, but in appearance the gap was much wider. She looked barely out of college and full of life and love and energy. I could feel her through the door, ready to bounce in and save the day, and I felt relieved because I knew I'd see Cindy on the other side of that door when I opened it.

And I did.

"What on earth is going on, Peter?" She burst into the house like a Tasmanian devil. "Hamilton is pissed. All the paperwork for the Brunswick Development is due tomorrow and you're not even in the office. I had to work through my lunch break trying to get caught up, and then I leave early to come check on you. We may have to go in at like five in the morning tomorrow if we're going to get it done in time for the planning meeting. Why are you still in your pajamas?"

"I just got up."

"At four in the afternoon?"

"I don't think so."

She stared at me for a minute, then looked around the room. "Strange, I thought you had a really high ceiling here, like ten feet or something."

"I did."

"What, you remodeled to make the place smaller? Who does that?"

I took her hand and pulled her down the hall, like a child wanting to show his mommy something. When we got to the doorway to the dining room I pointed and her eyes went to the black box. She shivered, like a chill had overcome her, and pulled back a little.

"It's disgusting," she whispered. "Obscene."

I felt strangely relieved. Someone else could not only see the box, but they could perceive that it wasn't just an ordinary box. It was something else, something disturbing.

"Where did it come from?" Cindy asked.

"I don't know."

She pulled her phone from her purse and brought it up like she was going to snap a picture of it, but the screen stayed dark. "My phone's dead. But I just charged it in the car, on the way here."

"Electronics don't seem to work near the box. I had to step out into the road before I could call you."

Cindy stepped into the dining room, edging step by step, ever closer to the box. She reached out to it, but instead of touching it directly, she tapped it with the edge of her phone. Sparks flew and she yelped as the phone burst into flames. She dropped it to the floor and we both stood and watched it burn. The case twisted and melted until it looked like it was in great pain, then the fire burnt itself out.

"That was not what I expected," Cindy said.

I nodded.

"That was a six-hundred-dollar phone."

"Sorry."

"Right. So, it doesn't like electronics. But the lights still work. So electricity isn't the problem. Circuit boards or microchips, maybe? Something like that?"

I thought about it. "The power strip in my bedroom stopped working. I don't think that has any circuit boards in it."

"Weird."

"Maybe it needs the light because it's so dark."

We stood there in silence for a while, watching the box as if it were some kind of dangerous animal. There was a complicated serious of deductions in my head but I couldn't figure out how to explain them. I couldn't even trace them all myself. Frustrated, I just blurted it out.

"I think it's eating my house."

Cindy glared at me. "What?"

"It may be eating time, too," I said.

"Why do you have to do that? As if that box isn't weird enough, you have to say something like that."

I pulled her back into the living room. "I didn't remodel anything, Cindy. The ceilings are lower than they were yesterday. And the room is smaller. It's all going away."

"That's impossible, Pete. Reality doesn't work like that."

"What time is it?" I asked.

"I don't know, my phone is a pile of molten goo!"

"Take a guess."

"About dinner time."

"Right, let's take a look." I pulled open the front door and we both looked outside. It was black as midnight.

Cindy looked at me like I was trying to trick her. "That's not possible," she said.

"Tell that to the box."

We closed the door and went back to the dining room. The box was still sitting there, silent and ominous. Flat black and featureless on all sides and yet I still had the impression that it was smiling at me.

Cindy started pacing back and forth, taking care to stay away from the box. I tried to ask her what she was thinking but she just held up a hand and ignored me. I watched, wondering how much time was ticking by. The rate could have been consistent, but I didn't think so. I suspect that it was speeding up all the time.

The dining room felt noticeably smaller now. I wondered what would happen when the room got too small for the table. In my mind I pictured the table starting to get crushed by the walls. That made me think of the trash compactor scene in Star Wars and in spite of everything that made me laugh.

Cindy stopped in her tracks and looked at me. I thought she was going to chide me for finding humor in the situation, but she just shook her head and said, "Ridiculous, isn't it?"

"It feels like it's all going to end here."

"All of what?" she asked.

"All of everything. Like this is the end of the world."

She looked back at the box. "It's like a black hole."

It was my turn to look shocked. "Black holes are in space."

"Yeah, but I've read about them. At least theory. They swallow up everything, whole planets, whole systems. And they say that time is distorted around them. That's what's happening here, right? It's eating the house and it's distorting time."

"I guess. But how does a black hole end up in a box?"

"Maybe the more important question is how the box ends up in your house."

"What do you mean?'

"Why you, Pete? What is it about you that would bring something like that here?" She gestured at the box and her voice became more animated. "If a black hole found its way into a box like that, that's one thing, and that's weird enough. But then it appears out of nowhere in the center of your dining room table.

Is it just happenstance, or is there something about here, or about you, that would draw it here?"

I thought about it, but I couldn't think of anything special, either about my home or about me. "I'm just a normal man living in a normal house."

"Are you, Pete?" She reached out and took my hand and held it in hers.

Her grip was warm and soft and I felt myself flush. I coughed nervously and she smiled at me. I had never really thought about it, but this was the first time since my divorce that I could remember consciously touching another human being. Was that possible? Could I have gone for years without any real contact with anyone? It seemed impossible.

But not as impossible as a black hole in my dining room.

"I've known you for years, Pete," she continued. "I'd say we were friends, but I don't think that's really true. Friends do things together, they have fun. When was the last time you had fun, Pete? When was the last time you enjoyed something, anything?"

"I don't remember," I whispered.

"You're kind of like a black hole yourself, Pete. It's like all joy disappears inside you and nothing is left but drudgery and routine. Perhaps it's drawn to you because of that."

"Oh c'mon!" I protested. "It's not like I'm the only unhappy person in the world. Do you have any idea how many people are on anti-depressants? If unhappiness is all it took there'd be a black hole box every half mile across the country."

Cindy opened her mouth to reply but before she could there was a tremendous crashing noise from the living room. She dropped my hand and we both rushed to see what had happened. The crashing sound had been a large book case that had been partially crushed as the ceiling had gotten lower still. That was only one of the changes, though, and perhaps the least alarming of them.

Sleight of Mind

The dimensions of the room had gotten noticeably smaller, not just in height but in width and depth. Oddly, some things seemed to have reduced in size along with the room, while others had not. The bookcase had still been its former height when the ceiling had crushed and toppled it, and the sofa appeared to be unchanged, while the coffee table was now smaller. The TV remained unchanged, but its stand had shrunk, making the TV appear much larger than it had been.

The windows had reduced in size along with the room, but the front door had not. It was crunched and partially folded and looked unlikely to ever open again. I walked to the window and looked out at my neighborhood. The sun was coming up now, but otherwise things looked pretty much the same.

"Maybe it's just the house," Cindy said. She was standing next to me at the window now, although I hadn't noticed her approach.

I shook my head. "No. I don't think so. I think the house is acting as a kind of seal, like a zip lock bag or something. But as soon as the house goes, it'll start pulling in everything out there."

"You don't think we can run from it?"

"I think if we open a window to get out, we'll break the seal and speed up the process."

"Shit."

"Yeah."

"Do you want the world to end?"

"No, of course not."

"Are you sure?"

I thought about it. "I guess I have found myself wishing that it was all over and done with. Life, I mean. Not in a suicidal way, I don't want to die, it's just that I don't really want to keep doing this, you know. It all seems so pointless."

Cindy took my hand again. "I think the box is you, Pete."

"Excuse me?"

"I think it's a manifestation of you and how you feel about life, without any of the complications. You're trying to turn everything off."

"I don't understand."

She pulled me over to the couch and we sat down. She kept hold of my hand. It felt nice, the first thing that had felt nice in a long time.

"How do you feel about me, Pete? Do you wish that I'd just turn off and go away?"

"No!" It came out louder and more forceful than I had intended. Apparently, it was something that I felt strongly about.

She smiled. "That's nice to hear. I think you're sweet, Peter. And you're kind of cute, too. One day, if the world survives, maybe we can explore that a little, although Hamilton might have a fit about it. But I don't think we can use that to bring you back, that's an awful lot of weight to put on a relationship."

"Bring me back?"

"To life. I think that's what this is really all about, Peter. I think that box is black and dead because that's what you're like inside now. I think you've let all the joy in you shrivel up and fade away and now you're letting the same thing happen to reality."

"How do we fix that?"

"I have an idea, but first we need to get outside. Hang on." She dashed into the kitchen and a moment later she was back with two glasses. "Window," she said.

I tried pulling the living room window open, but the frame had bent and it wouldn't budge. Cindy gestured for me to hurry up, so I grabbed an end table and pitched it through the glass. We knocked as many of the remaining shards loose as we could and then we carefully climbed out into the afternoon sun.

Cindy dashed for her car and I watched her rummage through her trunk and I felt something stir within me. It wasn't sexual, not then, but maybe it was affection. I hadn't felt anything but despair in so long that I had a hard time identifying it, but whatever it was, it felt good.

She came back to me with a bottle of wine, a corkscrew, and a giant box of cookies. "Supplies," she said, and grinned. "For my big night in. Netflix and chill all by myself, that was the plan. This is better, I think."

We sat in the grass on my front lawn and we drank and we ate and we enjoyed the sunny day. We talked about silly things and her laugh was both delightful and infectious. I knew this wasn't everything, that it might not last, and that the rest of the world was still waiting out there, ready to pounce. But as Cindy told me then, you take your joy where you can find it. On that fine sunny afternoon, a bottle of pinot grigio, a box of chocolate chip cookies, and Cindy's hand in mine was enough to save the world.

And maybe it was enough to save me.

(Not So) Dominant

The Great (or so he saw himself) Writer leaned back on his stool and exhaled a large cloud of cigarette smoke from his lungs.

He was on a stage in a small Irish pub in a small college town. He was there, of course, to say profound things. Why else would a Great Writer be on a stage?

He surveyed the crowd (not a large crowd, but not so tiny a crowd, either. not really) with careful eyes, absorbing details that lesser minds would miss, his keen intuitive nature picking up on subtle personality traits in his mostly young audience.

His mostly female audience.

A lesser mind make wonder about that, perhaps making an assumption that college males are much less likely to read books than their female counterparts. A lesser mind might even find that thought intriguing and wonder why it would be the case. Perhaps even run through some likely scenarios to explain such a thing.

But that was for a lesser mind.

The Great Writer's mind couldn't be bothered with such trivialities. It was too busy dissecting the subtle clues that would indicate which of the rapt young ladies would be the most likely to accompany him back to his hotel room. Which ones would be so awestruck by his brilliance that they would do anything he desired? Even the things they wouldn't do for their boyfriends.

It was a skill that rarely failed him.

But then, it was a rare night.

The girl he picked, the bookish little blonde with the pigtails and the tight, white sweater, the one who looked so sweet and adoring, who looked at him with those big blue eyes. Her thoughts were so much deeper, so much more profound than his own. She saw so easily through him, his (not so) subtle manipulations.

Tonight, he would do her bidding, she would have the control. He would cry, he would beg, he would be humiliated.

All there in that little college town, in that little Irish pub, for everyone to see.

....and he'd like it. The Great Writer would get a taste for it. Would look for it over and over again, in every town he visited, every stage he stepped upon. He'd always be looking for that bookish little blonde girl, to take control.

And he'd never turn that discerning eye inwards, never wonder why he longed for the humiliation, the loss of control.

And he'd never find such a girl again.

Regret

Why do so many monsters go by three names? John Wayne Gacy. Gary Leon Ridgway. Mark David Chapman. John Wilkes Booth. Lee Harvey Oswald.

Samuel Richard King.

I studied him through the one foot by one-foot plexiglass window set into the steel door that separated the free from the captive. Out here, I could change my mind, I could turn and leave, anytime I wanted. King didn't have that luxury. He'd never see the outside world again.

He was barely twenty-two years old, a small, nondescript man. His blonde hair was a little shaggy, but not exceptionally long. His complexion was just a little darkened from working outdoors, his hands callused but not very strong looking, as if the outdoor work was something new to him. According to my research, it was. He'd been working for a landscaping company a mere three weeks before it happened.

The only outward characteristic that hinted at what really lurked beneath were his eyes, dark and flat, like a two-dimensional drawing in an old comic book. They revealed nothing and perhaps revealed everything. Maybe only nothingness was there.

"I'm ready," I said, more to myself than to the guard that stood poised to let me into the interrogation room. I was there to interview King and even I wasn't sure why. I wasn't a true crime writer. I wrote paperback spy thrillers, the kind of book people bought at grocery stores and airports. I had spun some story about doing a feature article for a major magazine to the Gattlenburg District Attorney and he had believed me, partly because we had gone to High School together and partly because I was the most famous person to come out of Gattlenburg, which really tells you all you need to know about Gattlenburg, Maryland.

But no magazine had commissioned an article on Samuel Richard King. I was standing there of my own accord, desperate to speak to the man who had killed fourteen students and two teachers, with no real idea of what I hoped to learn.

The guard opened the door and I limped into the barren room, my bad knee jolting with every step. The cane that I normally relied on had been held at the front gate by a bored looking man with a clip board, presumably to prevent a prisoner from grabbing it and beating me to death. I pulled a notepad and pen from my jacket pocket as I sat down across from King.

"You're Daniel Hardwick?" he asked.

I nodded.

"My father has all your books. Had, I guess. I read one of them. Wasn't bad."

"Which one?"

He shrugged. "Had a clown in it. And some guys with a bomb in a suitcase."

"The Vernan Gambit."

"Whatever."

He didn't sound evil. There was a hard edge to his voice, but it was more petulant teenager than monster. Samuel Richard King had a clean record, not even a speeding ticket, until two weeks ago, when he walked into the local high school, a school we had both attended, and started shooting people.

"You going to write a book about me?" he asked.

"An article."

"Why?"

"You don't think your story is interesting enough for an article?"

He laughed. "Shit, I think I'm interesting enough for the movies. That's not what I meant. Why am I interesting to you?

There's what, a school shooting every couple of weeks in this country? Do you write articles on all of them?"

"No. Just the ones in my home town."

King laughed at that. "Like you're some hometown boy. You left here right after you got out of school, didn't you? What was that, thirty years ago?"

"A little more than that."

"How many times you been back?"

I stared at him for a moment, thinking about how to answer. I wasn't comfortable with the way the interview was going, but I still opted for honesty. "Once. For my father's funeral."

"How'd that go?"

"Not so well. My brother and I have... issues."

"So, you ain't been here in years and all of a sudden you're interested in what goes down in your home town? Smells like bullshit to me, man."

"Maybe I feel like I owe it something after all these years. Maybe I have some regrets."

"Why did you leave?"

"There was nothing else for me here. Gattlenburg is hardly a major center for publishing, especially back when there wasn't all this online stuff. Now you can write from anywhere and just email it off. Didn't used to work that way. Hell, I even wrote on a manual typewriter."

"Right. So, that's the rehearsed answer you've been giving everyone for thirty years. What's the real reason?"

I thought about it for the first time in a long time. He was right, of course, the answer I had given was well practiced and oft repeated. I didn't like thinking about it, about my past. After all those years, I still hadn't made my peace with life.

"My father," I said. "I left to get away from my father."

"Abusive?"

"Not really. Indifferent and judgmental, I guess."

"Odd combination."

"Yeah. He didn't put a lot of time or thought into what I did, he didn't pay much attention to me at all, but on the rare occasion he did, all I got was sarcasm and belittlement. He was a blue-collar guy, through and through, a construction foreman. He thought a man should do a man's job. So, two sons and he got a writer and a high school teacher."

"Your brother's a teacher?"

"He was."

I let the silence hang in the room. There was an elephant there now, and neither one of us wanted to look at it too closely.

When the silence got to be too much, he asked, "Just what do you think would have been different if you'd stayed in Gattlenburg?"

"I think I would have ended up at the school, also. Probably teaching English, or maybe Drama."

King thought about that for a moment and I could see the wheels turning behind those cold eyes, trying to find my angle. "Did you talk to your brother about that?" he asked.

"No. We hadn't talked in years. Since the funeral."

"Those issues you mentioned?"

"Yes."

"And that's one of the things you regret?"

I nodded. "Do you have any regrets?" I asked him. "Sixteen people are dead. How does that make you feel?"

"Powerful."

"And yet here you sit."

"S'not so bad. Three squares and a cot, guaranteed, for the rest of my life."

I shook my head. It wasn't what I had expected to hear. I was prepared for anger or perversion, perhaps even enjoyment. All of those are common emotional responses in serial and spree killers, all of them I could wrap my head around in some way. But King seemed indifferent.

Like my father.

"What is it you expect to happen here?" he asked. "What do you want out of this?"

"Forgiveness, I think."

"From me? I don't even know you. And I'm hardly the man to be handin' out absolution, not after what I've done. What is it you think you're responsible for? Not sticking around and gracin' our class with your presence? You think things would have turned out different if you were there?"

"I don't know."

"Then what is it you want forgiveness for? Walking away from your brother? I'm the man who killed him, how can I forgive you?"

"You didn't kill my brother, Samuel. He died of pancreatic cancer last night. He was in hospice care when you went on your spree. You did shoot his replacement, but he was one of the survivors."

"Then what is this? What do you want?"

"To understand why I had to leave. To understand why you had to kill those people."

"I couldn't leave. You got out, man. I couldn't. I don't have any talent, I was never going to be a writer, or an actor, or a singer. This was the only way."

"The only way for what?"

"To get famous. That's what getting out is all about, right? Fame and fortune?"

"Famous?"

"Like Gattlenburg's native son, the big shot writer man. Like you."

"Samuel, I made forty-two thousand dollars last year. Before taxes. I live in a rented townhouse in suburban New Jersey. No one asks for my autograph; I don't do book tours. I'm just a working writer. It's just another job."

He stared at me and I could see it on his face. He didn't believe me. He thought I was lying to him and he was trying to figure out why.

I stood up and turned from him. The weight of time and events bore down on me and it felt difficult to move. King wasn't what I expected him to be. He wasn't beaten down by the town and by the system. The school wasn't his oppressor. If he was the victim of anything it was reality television and the cult of celebrity.

Gattlenburg has always felt like a tragedy to me, and in some way that I'll never fully understand, it felt like a tragedy of my own making. Perhaps in my avoidance of my brother and of the town, they became the same thing to me. I wasn't there for either of them in their time of need. And while one had nothing to do with the other, in my mind they were also the same.

I looked back at King, expecting him to say something, but he remained silent as I left the cold, concrete room. Silent and disappointed.

Meat

"Who are you?" The Interrogator asked.

"No one." It came out in a quiet gasp. It was all He could manage now. It had been hours since He had sipped water, days since He had eaten.

"Everyone is someone," the Interrogator stated. Its voice was mechanical but it still managed to convey incredulity amidst the clicks and whirrs of its central processor.

"Not anymore," He whispered.

More buzzing and clicking came from the Interrogator. "Explain."

"We're leaving the system behind. No more names, no more numbers. If you can't catalogue us, you can't control us."

"Your logic is faulty."

"I have no logic, I am meat."

The Interrogator smiled as it raised his arm and shot a bolt of electricity through Him, killing Him instantly.

It clicked and whirred as it filled out the disposal form, under the entry for name it put the word "Meat".

Sympathy

"Did you sleep the sleep of the just?" The well-dressed man asked.

I looked around the little room and took in its bare walls and simple furnishings. There wasn't even a window. I sat on the edge of a neatly kept cot. He sat on a wooden chair.

"Where am I?" I asked.

"Ah," he replied. "So that's how it's going to be. You are in your room."

I looked around again. The statement was absurd. I didn't recognize the room; how could it be mine? Yet, I couldn't recall what my own room should look like. How could that be the case?

The well-dressed man was smiling. "Do you remember anything? Do you remember your name? Or mine?"

I didn't. The realization startled me, but I remembered absolutely nothing before waking just minutes ago. I said, "No," then waited anxiously for him to tell me, to pierce the dark cloud that hung over my memory.

"Let's take a different tact," he said. "How do you feel?"

I thought about it. "I feel fine," I answered. "I am tired, like the night was long and full of strenuous work, but physically my body feels strong. I have no particular aches or pains of which to complain."

He nodded and continued to smile. "Look at your hands. Examine them."

I found I didn't want to do as he said. Something about his smile was bringing dread to my heart. I had to force myself to look down at my hands. They were thin and pale and etched with lines.

"Your fingernails," he whispered. "Look closely."

There were dark stains under the edges of my nails. I examined them closely, the dread creeping up on me. "Blood?" I asked.

"Yes, very good. And how do you feel, now?"

I felt like my nerves would surely tear me apart. The fear and the dread had a firm grip on me. They would do their work and they would do it well.

"Fine," I answered. "I feel fine."

"Of course, you do." The well-dressed man stood from his chair and stepped closer to me for just a moment. I thought he was going to touch me and the very thought chilled me to the bone. He was so close that I felt sure that I would feel his breath upon my cheek but I felt nothing.

"When do you think it is," he whispered.

"When?" I replied, puzzled by the question.

"What year do you believe it to be?"

"I don't know."

"What decade?"

"I... I don't know."

"What century is it, do you think?"

I shook my head violently. "I don't know. Please, stop."

"Oh, that's ironic," he said. He was back in his chair now, sitting comfortably. Watching. "She used those same words. Remarkable."

"Who?"

"I'm getting ahead of myself. We'll get there, don't you worry."

I found myself shivering and realized that the temperature in the room felt like it had dropped by several degrees in the last few moments. I looked at the well-dressed man, but he showed no sign of discomfort.

"Who are you?" I asked.

"Guess."

"I really have no idea. Are you a doctor?" I looked about the room once more. "Am I in a hospital? Or an asylum?"

"Not this time."

"This time?" I asked, growing frustrated.

"We have danced this dance before, you and I. So many times. But the result is always the same. You seek to cleanse your hands but you can never cleanse your soul."

I looked right at him, but I did not see him. Instead, I saw my hands again, covered in blood, certain that the blame was not mine to bear.

"You are no priest," I said.

"No," he agreed. "I am far from that."

"I have done nothing wrong," I said.

"You're sure of that? With no memory of what happened, this time or the times before, you are still sure that the blood on your hands is not of your doing? Remarkable."

The room felt even colder. I could feel his indignation like a tangible presence in the room. Even worse, I could feel my mind beginning to open, and I knew that whatever it held in its dark recesses, I wanted no part of it.

"You were there," I whispered. "You urged me to turn away. You said it was not my concern."

"Of course, I did," he replied. "That's what I do. That's what I've always done."

"Then why do you torment me now?"

"Because you feel no guilt," he said, and for the first time I heard the anger in his voice.

"I did nothing wrong." The memories were flooding back. Not just from this time, but from all the times before.

"You let them hang an innocent man. You knew that he had done nothing wrong and you let them take him anyway. Even as his wife pleaded for you to stop them."

"There was nothing I could have done. They would have taken him regardless of my decision." I felt the weight behind my words.

"You've used that same argument in your defense for centuries. You used it in Germany. You used it in Russia. You used it in the court of Kings. And you used it in Judaea."

"It was not my fault."

"How do you bear this burden, Pontius? I tire of playing this eternal game with you, I want your guilt and I want your damned soul. The blame is yours."

"I wash my hands of this," I said.

"Of course, you do," he replied. "You always wash your hands of it. That is the reason that we keep ending up in this room, you and I. You take no responsibility."

"I WASH MY HANDS OF THIS!" I shouted.

And the well-dressed man was gone. I looked down at my hands. They were clean, even under the edges of my nails.

I stood and walked from the room, out into the brightness of a new day. A new beginning.

Whiskey Delirium

It's 2AM, and the whiskey has done its work.

I can still hear the dead outside, walking around, scratching at the doors and windows, but I no longer care. I've managed to drink away the last of my survival instinct. It went down cold and bitter, like the Tequila once did.

I miss Tequila.

The cameras on the wall still follow my every move. I suspect they're programmed now. No one left alive to control their movements. Not in this world.

The light outside the window is bright. Too bright for the middle of the night. The sun doesn't work anymore, anyway.

It's a trick, it has to be. I wonder who's behind it. I don't think the dead are that clever. Maybe I'll ask the one who brings my pills. It should be along, soon. It's been nearly three hours.

You don't have to tell me, you know. I realize that I'm not all right. There's something wrong inside my head. Things no longer track.

Would you be okay in these circumstances? If the dead walked and the sun refused to shine and a decomposing nurse brought you little blue pills every three hours? I didn't think so.

Dammit, the whiskey is wearing off.

Where are my clothes?

Shuffle

Memory is not a continuous stream or a single tapestry. It's a series of individual moments and events, stitched together like scenes in a movie. Imagine trying to make sense of your life if those scenes were shuffled like a deck of cards. Over and over again.

Shuffle.

It's morning. I'm in a disgusting hotel room that looks like it hasn't seen maid service in a year or two. The furniture is stained and

I'm trying not to think about what made the stains. Everything is dark, the light bulbs are covered in a thick coat of nicotine. The blinds block out most of the sunlight, except where they've cracked and crumbled with age.

I remember checking in here. It was the night my wife threw me out. I want to say that it was fifteen years ago, by now. I can't. My mind no longer works that way. I have to piece things together like a puzzle. Separate events from their perceived order and build them into a logical timeline.

All the while, wondering if any of the pieces to the puzzle are missing. There's just no way to tell.

This can't be the night after my wife threw me out. That's impossible. I still remember her murder, whenever it happened. A week ago, a year ago. It doesn't matter. She couldn't have thrown me out after she was murdered. No way to make that work on the timeline.

So, I'm here again. Back in the same shitty hotel room. Have they even changed the sheets? Why would I come back here? Isn't this where...?

Shuffle.

I'm in the hospital. They've got me hooked up to all sorts of machines. They all make faint little beeping noises. I'm strapped to the bed. Can't have me getting up and walking away. I feel like I'm floating. Probably the morphine. I think I was shot in the head.

Molly is in a chair in the corner. She's been crying for a long time. Somehow, that makes me feel a little better. She always looks so damn perfect. It's nice to see her makeup run. I don't think she's crying for me, anyway.

This can't be now. I remember getting better from this. I remember healing. I remember fighting with Molly and her going away.

I remember the hotel room.

Shuffle.

Knock, Knock. Pound! Pound!

"Open up in there, Mr. Devlin."

Yeah, this hotel room. This disgusting hole of a room. I think it might be my home. I wonder about the man outside. His voice doesn't sound familiar. I start to reach for the door and notice the bruises on my hands. I've hit someone recently.

Blood on my sleeve. What have I done, now? Do I remember it? Some violent event shuffled into my past? He knocks again, but I stay very quiet. I hope he'll go away. I hope I haven't done anything too awful.

There's a long pause, then a huge thud and a cracking noise as the wood splinters. I go… Elsewhen.

Shuffle.

I'm in a bar in East Lansing. It's full of college students. Most of them are pretty. One of them is stunning. A tall redhead, with perfect legs. She's wearing a mini skirt and I can't take my eyes off of her.

She buys me a drink. Tells me she has a thing for older guys. Especially married ones. I shake my head. "Separated," I tell her.

"Even better." Her name is Molly. She's wearing a wedding ring, too. I don't ask about it. That was probably a mistake. I make a lot of those.

Shuffle.

The phone is ringing.

I'm in another hotel room, but this one is much nicer. Clean sheets, room service cart against the wall. There's an empty bottle of champagne on top of the cart, along with two glasses. There's a naked woman in bed, her head resting against my shoulder as she sleeps.

I can't see who she is. The angle is wrong.

I answer the phone. It's Molly.

"Jamie, what have you done?" She screams. "What have you done?"

My hands are battered and bruised. The woman feels cold beside me.

Shuffle.

I'm in prison. It's rare for me to be able to connect cause and effect. But in prison, they tell you why you're here. They do it to shame you, although some prisoners seem to wear that knowledge like a badge of honor.

I'm here because I killed Molly's husband. I remember doing it, although it seems like it was a long time ago, long before I met Molly. Impossible, I know. I have to keep thinking about the timeline.

It was an accident; I didn't mean to hurt him. Not like...

They called it accidental manslaughter. I was defending myself. Neither of us saw the stairway. Either of us could have died in the fall. It just turned out to be him.

Shuffle.

I'm standing in the atrium of Molly's building. I'm on parole.

She never visited while I was inside. She said it was over, that she couldn't handle any more of the craziness. Of my craziness.

I'm pleading with her to give me another chance. I tell her that I love her more than anything.

Then there's a cracking noise. It startles us both. I can feel something warm and sticky running down the side of my face. I go to wipe it away and I see the look of abject terror in Molly's eyes.

She starts to scream.

Shuffle.

It's my first day outside of the hospital. Molly is explaining the damage the bullet did to my brain. The doctors have explained it to me before, but I can never remember it right.

Molly tells me that it was just bad luck. A drive-by shooting.

I don't believe her. But I smile and nod in all the right places. She kisses me and tells me that everything is going to be okay.

I think she knows better.

Shuffle.

I've just run into my wife in the hotel bar. She has a suite upstairs. She's back in town for a meeting with a client.

I already knew all of that.

She's drunk and she keeps apologizing to me. She won't say what she's apologizing for, but I know.

It's not enough.

She asks me if I'd like to come back to her room with her. For old time's sake. She puts her hand over mine and smiles.

Shuffle.

Molly's voice, on the phone. "What did you do? My god, Jamie, what did you do?"

Shuffle.

Sleight of Mind

The cold woman at my side, she's not breathing. I think that's my fault. And I think I know who she is.

Shuffle.

The sound of splintering wood.

Two men burst through the door and into the squalid room. They have guns pointed at me.

"You're very young," I say. "You look nervous."

"Don't you fucking move," says the one in front. I don't. I let them cuff me and lead me from the room.

They say things. Lots of things. Most of them slip away so fast. One echoes in my head, over and over.

"You're under arrest for the murder of Jennifer Devlin."

Did I do it? I can't remember.

But I think it fits the timeline.

Actually, Mr. Benedict

"So why run?"

It was the first thing in the morning, and here was this reporter, right on his doorstep, and she was asking him that. Of all things, she asks that.

"So, it's out, huh. I thought I got away clean. Damn. I guess everything's over. Why run? So I wouldn't get caught, that's why. Do you know what this means? What it does to me?

"I'm finished. You're here now, but I'm sure the police will be right behind you. I can't explain it, can't talk my way out of it. I ran. They were all shouting, identifying themselves, ordering me to stop.

Have you ever been in that situation? It's terrifying. I panicked. I admit it, I panicked.

"I don't even know what I was doing there in the first place. I mean, it's not like it was a habit or anything. I never set foot in the place until last night. Bob talked me into it. We had been drinking, neither of us had ever done anything like that before, it seemed like a lark.

"God knows, we never expected the place to be raided. Place has been running for years, right out in the open like that, first time it gets raided is the one and only night I'm there. How's that for luck?

"And we certainly didn't know the girl was underage. I mean yeah, she looked a little young, but I figured, she must be eighteen. They wouldn't let her work there unless she was eighteen. Then she tells us she's fifteen. Can you imagine? Right in the middle of, well, you get the idea.

"And before I can react, before I can even comprehend what she just said, blam, here they are, yelling and screaming, waving guns. So, I grabbed my pants and hauled ass. What would you have done? Stayed and let yourself be ruined? Of course not. You'd have taken off, too.

"I bet it was Bob, wasn't it? He must have got caught and spilled the beans. Told everyone I was there so he'd get off the hook. That son of a bitch. It was Bob, wasn't it?"

The reporter smiled, a grin bigger than any he'd ever seen before. I grin like the proverbial cat who swallowed the canary. And she said the most remarkable thing.

She said, "Actually, Mr. Benedict, I was asking why you had chosen to run for Congress."

In The Court of The Yellow King

The house was painted a dull yellow, like it had been left too long in the sun and all of its vibrance and life had faded away. It sat far back from the road, alone. Forest surrounded it on three sides, but even the trees seemed to keep their distance, leaving a barren space of dirt and twigs around it. The windows were cloudy with decades of grime that obscured everything within except for the faint glow of the lights and the battered and broken window blinds which were always pulled half-way down. The house had no neighbors to speak of. It sat on a seldom used road, three miles north of the Ilchester Tunnel, so to say that no one ever saw another human being enter or leave the house isn't saying much, but still.

No one ever saw the solitude of the yellow house disturbed, not by man or beast. It was better that way. The things that happened in that dull yellow house were never meant to be seen. Not by human eyes. I wish with all my heart that I was not the exception that proved that rule, that I had never seen that house, that I had never set foot upon its land, much less inside the dreaded thing. Wishes are devilous things, they often come far too late, and they are granted only by things better left in the recesses of imagination and the corner of the eye.

Even knowing that, if I had the opportunity to make such a wish now, if I could turn back the clock so that I had never come down to the state of Maryland, I would offer up any sacrifice necessary. I would never have opened the letter from St. Mary's College, never agreed to come and provide a guest lecture in the folklore that was my specialty, if I had known any of what was to follow.

I suppose I should have been concerned with the specificity of the request, the origin of an otherworldly phantom known as a flimmern-geist and the details of the dimension it inhabits when not being brought forth into our own. I had to forage through quite a few arcane books from my private library to find any answers as the flimmern-geist is an obscure spirit even in my area of expertise. After pushing past several brief references in various guides, I found a more detailed explanation in a volume by a sixteenth century alchemist named Jakob Bohme.

Bohme was a Lutheran Mystic of the time and much of his work involved blending folklore with religious dogma. He believed that a flimmern-geist was the spirit of someone who had died a violent death and spent eternity in a place just beyond the edge of our vision. His work was unclear on just what that place might be, although there was some allusion to purgatory or someplace very like it.

That brought something to mind and sent me digging for another volume that I had obtained some years previous. It was without a title and badly translated from Arabic, but it mentioned an ancient and cursed city on the shores of a Lake Hali that lies just beyond the edge of our vision. The phrasing, in translation at least, was exact. It could be coincidence, but my mind leapt with excitement at the connection, a feeling that perhaps only dusty old academics like I would understand.

With these finds, I had enough information that I could feel comfortable speaking on the subject, but more importantly, the request had left me with the impression that I might learn even more if I could exchange thoughts with the group that had requested my lecture. In the end, it was my own thirst for knowledge that had me sending an affirmative reply and packing my bags for the train ride down from Kingsport, Massachusetts.

It was still early into the new century and even though 1910 felt like a progressive new time to us, the faculty at my college were concerned about sending a female professor off on such an adventure on her own. But we were a small institution and I was paying for the trip out of my own funds, hoping to replace the hole in my account with the offered speaking fee, so in the end, I left in my own company.

When I arrived in Ellicott City, I took a room in the Howard House Hotel, a towering structure built into the side of a granite hill, overlooking Main Street. The train ride had left me exhausted, so I had an early dinner there at the hotel and went back to my room to sleep. There I dreamt of black stars over a still lake. I awoke in the morning feeling refreshed but uneasy.

St. Mary's College was just over two miles from the hotel, but it was a pleasant spring day and I decided to walk there, hoping that the Sister Haversham who had written me would be free to talk upon my arrival. I was in no hurry and my walk was a leisurely one, and yet I found myself becoming anxious as I went. The people I passed were outwardly friendly, but I sensed something else, an undercurrent of suspicion, or perhaps something darker.

I would have dismissed it as mere paranoia, brought on by my journey and the strange dreams that followed, were it not for what happened when I arrived at the college. There was no Sister Haversham there, they had never heard of her. I showed them the letter that had been sent and, although it appeared to be on authentic stationary, the folklore class that it mentioned did not exist. It all appeared to be an elaborate practical joke, one that had cost me a great deal of money.

I walked back to the hotel in a dazed silence. The loss of the funds that I had expended thus far was upsetting, but not debilitating. While I was not a wealthy woman, my grandfather had left me enough money that I could live comfortably as I pursued my academic interests.

It was the mystery behind the entire thing that nagged at my mind. My initial thoughts about being the victim of a joke seemed less likely the longer I considered the matter. The knowledge required to compose that initial letter was so arcane that even I, an expert in world folklore, had to research what was described. The very idea that a layman would have such information at their fingertips was ridiculous.

I was greeted back at the hotel by a message that a Mr. Cornelius Haversham was in the lounge, awaiting my return. It appeared that I would get some answers after all. Mr. Haversham was a large man with a bushy beard and hands the size of hams. He rose from his spot to greet me and as he took my hand, I found his touch to be light and his voice surprisingly gentle.

"My sincere apologies, Professor. I had hoped to catch you before you left for St. Mary's, but it appears that I missed you by a quarter of an hour."

"I see," I said, curtly. "I suppose that effort is at least somewhat commendable, but it doesn't excuse the false claims that brought me here."

"No, I suppose it doesn't, but those claims are not as false as they appear. Please, join me, and I'll try to explain."

I sat down, hoping that I appeared reluctant. In truth, I was finding the whole thing utterly fascinating and I could not wait to hear more.

"I represent a private organization with a great interest in certain elements of folklore. Everything in the letter that we sent to you was of genuine interest. We very much do want you to speak on the subject and we will happily pay you for your time. We just thought that you would take our request more seriously if it came from the college."

"A private organization?"

"Yes. We call ourselves the Knights of the Yellow Court."

"And the letter I received? I would imagine it to be foolish to declare a written hand to be definitely masculine or feminine, yet I have a hard time imaging your heavy hands producing so delicate a script. Is there, indeed, a Sister Haversham?"

He smiled, briefly, and, I think, almost laughed. "I don't think anyone would mistake dear Margaret for a bride of Christ, but I do have a sister and it was she who wrote the letter, or at least it was in her hand. I suppose we all composed it, by committee, as it were."

"And just what is your committee's interest in flimmern-geists?"

Haversham's face changed, almost imperceptibly, as if he was trying carefully to remember a well-rehearsed speech. "There's a local story, a legend. About a man named Thom. It's said that he was killed in the final blast that made the Illchester Tunnel."

"Said?"

"No body was ever found. No trace at all, no blood, no bone, nothing.

"What do you believe happened to him?" I asked.

"We think he was blown into another world. That he became a flimmern-geist.

"Existing just beyond human vision?"

"Yes. Visible only through the corner of your eye," he said. "Have you ever heard of Carcosa?"

"It doesn't sound familiar."

"Strange is the night where black stars rise

And strange moons circle through the skies

But stranger still

Is lost Carcosa."

I thought of the black stars over the lake in my dream and a shiver ran through me. "I think," I said, "that you should take me to meet the rest of your yellow knights."

Haversham shook his hefty head. "I wish that I could. For one, our meeting hall is under construction at the moment. There was a minor flood, it caused some structural damage." Then he laughed, nervously. "And most of the others aren't around right now. They didn't believe you'd come."

"I see."

"But Doctor Henning is in town. He's our chief officer. He has a home up on College Road. It's a sizeable place, we could gather those who could come and meet there."

My enthusiasm for the subject was getting the better of me, but an undercurrent of unease had settled in and taken hold of my heart. I could feel it pounding, not in excitement, but in dread, somehow understanding the danger of my situation in a way that my conscious mind did not.

If I could have seen the faded yellow house where Mr. Haversham was suggesting we meet, I think, even not knowing what lay ahead, I would have turned him down, enthusiasm be damned. Such was the power of that place, that it made clear it's horrible intent with just a glimpse.

But here, in the safety of the hotel lounge, my undefined discomfort was not enough to dispel my curiosity and I agreed to meet with the remnants of his group that very evening. We settled on a time and it was arranged that Margaret Haversham would be at the front of the hotel with a carriage to take me to Doctor Henning's home, where I would give my initial presentation to the few members of the Court who were available to gather.

I spent the rest of that afternoon napping, and I dreamt once more of the black stars over the still and quiet lake. This time, on the distant shore, I could see the silhouette of a man, tall and thin, wearing a tall hat. He stood perfectly still at the edge of the water, but I could sense that he was waiting for something. In the final moments, before I woke, I heard a horrible voice whisper to me.

"Don't close your eyes," it said. "Open the door."

I awoke in a fevered sweat, and took my time preparing for the evening's work. I bathed there in the hotel, although the water felt old to me, and somehow unclean. I dressed neatly in the finest outfit that

I had brought with me, one that my students back home had called matronly, but in an admiring way. I was just three years shy of my fiftieth birthday and I had never married. Few men had ever called me beautiful, but matronly, to my ear, sounded respectful, if not complimentary, and it was, I suppose, what I felt was a well-earned description.

Satisfied with my appearance, I sat at the room's elegant desk and studied my notes until the agreed upon time. It wasn't until I was headed down to the lobby that I even considered food. There was no time now, I could see my carriage waiting on the street outside. I almost turned back then, telling myself it was out of hunger and not fear, for the very sight of the carriage had set my nerves afire. But I was a distinguished academic with the greatest knowledge of folklore on the eastern seaboard, and I would not be frightened off by a missed meal and a little girl's flutters.

Margaret Haversham was waiting for me in the carriage, a stern looking woman of about my age, perhaps a few years younger. She nodded at me, but remained largely silent during our journey. I tried to engage her in conversation, but got little more than indifferent mutters in reply. If she had any interest in my presence or in what I had to tell her organization, she hid it well.

It took our carriage just over half of an hour to reach the yellow house. I looked at it, sitting there in the woods, in all its malevolence, and I felt my resolve seep away. It looked old and in disrepair, but that couldn't account for the atmosphere of sheer horror that surrounded the place. As I stepped from the carriage, I found myself shivering, as though the temperature had dropped significantly during our ride.

I looked to Margaret, hoping for some sign of encouragement, but found instead a face void of emotion, flat and disinterested. I looked back at the house and saw it, not through the fog of my initial response but simply as it was, a small, yellow house that had seen better days. Indicating, perhaps, an impoverished organization with a dwindling membership, like so many similar historical organizations back in New England. Not frightening, I told myself, but sad. And having convinced myself that my misgivings were just a leftover effect of my eerie dreams, I made the biggest mistake of my life.

I stepped inside.

The group that waited for us within was small, just three men including Haversham, and one woman. The neatest and most professional looking of the men turned out to be the house's owner, Doctor Clifford Henning. He greeted me and introduced the remaining members, a husband and wife named Frank and Dorothy Copper.

The living room was set up for an informal presentation, with the five members of the Court taking their seats on a pair of well-worn settees, positioned in a 'v'-shape. A coffee table sat before them and several glasses sat upon it, half drunk. The doctor and Mr. Cooper both reached for their glasses as they sat. At the front of the room was an old lectern, and I stepped behind it and took a deep breath, attempting to steady my shaken nerves.

Sleight of Mind

A woman whom I had not seen before, and assumed to be Doctor Henning's house keeper, stepped into the room and brought me what appeared to be a glass of spirits. I took it, gratefully, and took a sip before I began, savoring the smoky taste of the whiskey. I talked of flimmern-geists for over an hour, drinking two full glasses of whiskey in the process, to calm my nerves. I covered the history of the term itself and the legends surrounding both how a flimmern-geist was created and where it resided when it was not menacing someone on the earthly plane. That was the area that seemed to spark the most interest in the group.

"This place they inhabit," Doctor Henning asked, "is it accessible from our world?"

"The method of doing so varies according to culture," I replied. "But certainly. One medieval European tome references human sacrifice. More recent volumes suggest some sort of ritual, usually involving vision."

"Vision?" Mrs. Copper inquired.

"Yes. Because the flimmern-geist exists in a realm visible from the corner of the eye, finding a way into that realm inevitably involves entering through that vision. A Germanic volume from the 15th century suggests removing the eyes altogether, but Jakob Bohme believed that you could open the doorway by staring, unblinking, for a period of time."

"For how long?" Again, from Doctor Henning.

"A significant but not impossible amount of time. It's not specified in the work, but these sorts of stories are usually vague. I suspect that it's more important that the length is meaningful to the practitioner. Folklore suggests that ritual or spell is more about achieving a state of mind than following a precise set of instructions. Perhaps an hour would be appropriate, but I imagine that even an hour would be close to impossible to actually achieve."

Now that my presentation itself had drawn to a close, I could feel the whiskey going to my head. I wanted nothing more than to ask Margaret Haversham to return me to my hotel, but my audience still had questions they were determined to ask.

"Where would such a ritual have to take place?"

"I think that would vary depending on the flimmern-geist you were attempting to reach. The best place would be where the spirit had met its violent end, I suppose. Could I sit down, I really am feeling very light headed."

"Of course, you are," Henning said, taking me by the arm and guiding me to the couch. "That would be the laudanum." I tried to pull away in alarm, but my muscles no longer seemed to be responding to my commands. The faces of my hosts seemed to be distorting in horrible ways, shimmering and dissolving in the gaslight.

"Please," I mumbled, but found myself unable to finish the thought. I sought out Margaret's eyes and found them to be smiling in a hideous fashion. It was there, in her eyes, that I finally realized the full implications of my peril, and knew that there was absolutely nothing I could do to help myself. I was falling into the deepest blackness I had ever experienced and the last thing that I heard as I fell, filled me with an exquisite terror.

"Prepare my surgery…"

I woke outside, unable to move, my entire body racked with pain. I was strapped to a wooden framework, standing before a dark tunnel. The skin around my eyes felt unnaturally tight and I found that I couldn't close them. A wooden block was pressed against either side of my head, so that I couldn't turn my neck to look around.

I tried to voice a question, to ask where I was, what had been done to me, but all that came out was a harsh croak. A voice spoke softly beside me, the now chilling voice of Doctor Henning.

"Don't try to speak. You are dehydrated from the procedure. You'll just do yourself further harm."

My eyes ached and itched and I tried desperately to force my lids closed, to no avail. Henning walked around in front of me and smiled.

"Let me." He held up a glass dropper and let its liquid fall into my eyes, each in turn. It felt soothing, and I fought back the ridiculous urge to thank him for his kindness. "You are probably wondering where you are, yes?"

I nodded as best I could with the confines of my restraints.

"This is the entrance to Illchester Tunnel, finished by the B&O railroad just seven years ago. It is where Black Thom is said to have lost his life, in the final explosion that cleared the tunnel. It is Thom that haunts this place, Thom that brings us here tonight. There is a story that has begun to circulate, that if you can stare into the mouth of this tunnel for an hour, as you yourself suggested, unblinking, then you can open a doorway and let Thom through. Once you've seen him, though, well, he becomes attached. Each time you close your eyes after that, he gets just a little closer. The only way to hold him at bay is to refrain from blinking completely."

There I heard Mr. Haversham laugh. "You don't have to worry about that part, Professor," he said. "The doctor has sown your eyelids open, you see. You cannot blink. So, Thom will not be able to harm you."

I became aware that the rest of Henning's murderous group was there, unseen, behind me. I couldn't see anything but the tunnel in front of me and I wondered how long I had left, how long I had been staring into the darkness.

My body tensed and tried to recoil in horror, but it could not move. What felt like leather straps bound me expertly to the wood. I could only see in front of me, down the darkened tunnel, but my vision was adjusting to the darkness, and with the full moon in the sky it seemed that I could now see through to the other side.

"You are wondering, why?" Henning asked.

I mouthed the word 'yes' as carefully as I could, and the Doctor nodded.

"Of course, you are," he said. "It must seem unfathomable to you. We have no interest in meeting Black Thom, we shall leave that pleasure for you. Our interest is entirely in what lies on the other side of that doorway. You spoke briefly with Mr. Haversham, I believe, about lost Carcosa. It is an ancient city on the shore of the black Lake Hali, not far from fabled Hastur. During the day it is lit by twin suns, and by night it is circled by strange moons. It is ruled over by a King in Yellow, whom we have served faithfully for many years. It is our destiny to join his court in Carcosa, so we have searched for many years to find the way there."

"You shall open the doorway for us," Margaret said. "When Thom comes through, we shall slip past him, into that ancient land."

I fought hard against the dryness in my cracked throat and managed to whisper, "why me?"

"There seems to be one more vital component to the ritual. Belief. We have tried this experiment twice before, but our offerings didn't understand, they didn't believe the gateway would open, therefore it did not. We decided that our next attempt should be someone who understood the ritual in a way that would brook no disbelief. Your background as an expert in this sort of folklore made you the perfect candidate."

From that point onward, Henning fell silent, like the others. He stepped back from my view and left me to my own horrified contemplation. Every few minutes, he would step forward and drop liquid into my eyes, to keep them from drying out in the night air. The world nearest me seemed to fall from focus and the end of the tunnel become sharp in my vision. I could see the trees gently moving in the breeze outside the end of it.

What felt like an eternity later was marked first by footsteps, then by the blurry sight of the five Knights of the Yellow Court making their way down to the far end of the tunnel and taking up their places alongside its inner walls.

I knew then that it wouldn't be much longer.

It started as a shimmering, like a dark reflection on a pool of water. Then I could see the lake from my dreams, and the darkly gleaming city beyond. A figure stepped forward, no longer on the far side but on the closest shore, and water dripped from his tall, tilted hat as he stepped into the tunnel.

He stood there, in the pale light, and as the Knights stepped through the doorway the world seemed to blink, in and of itself. They were no longer stepping onto the shore of Lake Hali. Now the vision through the end of the tunnel showed me that damned yellow house, and as the Knights stepped through, they screamed in horror, a scream unlike anything I had ever heard, a scream I felt in my very bones and organs.

Thom stood there in the tunnel, unmoving, as I watched Doctor Henning and his friends torn to bloody shreds by nothing, watching the blood and meat fly from their bodies like bits of mud and tree branch in a storm. Even amidst all the flying gore, the house remained untouched, it's yellow color almost iridescent now, in the darkness.

Sometime after that, the world darkened. I lost consciousness along with the last of my hope, and fell into a dreamless nothingness. I don't know how long I was gone, but the world was bright when I woke, and I was on the ground along the side of the tunnel. It was a train rumbling through that woke me and I watched it in utter disbelief that something so normal could still exist in this world.

My body was no longer bound! Someone (or something) had loosened my straps and freed me, although my eyes were still held firmly open and had dried out to the point that my vision was cracked and painful. I got to my feet and stumbled away from the tunnel, but not before one final look down that menacing tunnel.

In its darkness, I could still see the shape of Black Thom, standing there, waiting patiently for me to blink.

Sleight of Mind

That was two days ago. I'm back in the yellow house, now. It was a three-mile walk from the tunnel, but I encountered no one along the way. Not that it matters, no one could help me now.

I expected to find the housekeeper here, but she is gone. The place holds no signs of life but mine own. My eyes remain open and will stay that way until the end. It's the only way to keep him out there, at the edge of my vision. I apply the drops as frequently as I can remember, but truth to tell, it no longer seems to matter. The damage seems permanent.

I leave this record to warn others. I don't know how long I'll be able to maintain things as they are. I expect I may have another day or so, but it may be only hours. Once I'm gone, I think Thom will return to the other side, as long as no one is foolish enough to repeat the ritual. But I've been looking through Doctor Henning's papers and it looks like there are other disciples of the Yellow King, and I can only hope they read this before trying to find their way through to lost Carcosa.

The King in Yellow is a mad king, do not follow him into the darkness. Let Carcosa stay lost and let Black Thom rest under the black stars.

www.ingramcontent.com/pod-product-compliance
Lightning Source LLC
Chambersburg PA
CBHW031026260626
47153CB00017B/2281